Ex Libris

## "You spend your evenings together."

Ross's voice was accusing and Jenny nodded silently, close to tears.

"During the day Andrew is out climbing," Ross went on relentlessly. "That's why during the day you don't mind being with me."

"No, Ross," she protested.

"Yes, Ross," he said mockingly. "Oh, Jenny, I know how it is. I saw the way Andrew kissed you."

"Ross," she said very quietly, "Andrew was the one who did the kissing."

"I didn't see you struggle very hard to stop him," he said bitterly. "You're like all the other flirts I've met. How many men do you have on a string? Andrew and me...and Neil Donaldson...."

"You're not being fair," she said furiously.

"No." He pulled her close suddenly. "Shall I kiss you now, my dear, the way you were kissed by him?"

# *Harlequin Premiere Editions*

# Harlequin Premiere Editions

## FORESTS OF THE DRAGON

### Rosemary Carter

# Harlequin Books

TORONTO • LONDON • LOS ANGELES • AMSTERDAM
SYDNEY • HAMBURG • PARIS • STOCKHOLM • ATHENS • TOKYO

Original hardcover edition published in 1976
by Mills & Boon Limited

ISBN 0-373-82112-3

This Harlequin Premiere Editions volume
published October 1981

Printed in U.S.A.

# CHAPTER ONE

'Jenny.' The question came again. 'Will you go?'

'Lynn . . .' Jenny Windham raised troubled eyes to her friend. After a moment she bent her head once more and began to pour the tea. She put a cup of tea and a plate of scones on a table beside Lynn, then dropped on to a cushion near the fire. 'I don't know,' she said at last.

'You'd love it, Jenny. I know you would.' Lynn Ramsden watched the small slender girl, and wondered what she could say to convince her that the holiday would do her good. Jenny's fair hair looked like burnished gold, and her lovely violet eyes were almost black in the firelight. But her face was drawn, and a little too thin, and beneath her eyes tiredness and grief had etched small lines. With sun and fresh air and the relaxed environment of a mountain holiday, those lines would vanish, Lynn thought. 'Mom wants you to come, Jenny. She's so fond of you.'

'And I'm fond of her.' Jenny looked up swiftly. 'She's a dear. I'm so glad that she's better again.'

'Yes, she *is* better. But she needs a change of

climate. The doctor wants her to get away as soon as she can.'

'Yes . . .'

'I want someone to be with her, Jenny. If you won't agree to go I'll have to find somebody else.' Lynn paused and took a sip from her cup. 'It would be a holiday for you, Jenny. Mom doesn't need a nurse—you've had enough of nursing anyway. What she needs is a companion, a friend. And I know she wants it to be you.'

'But South Africa is so far away,' Jenny murmured, crumbling a piece of scone between her fingers.

'No more than a day by plane.'

'What did you say the mountains are called?'

'The Drakensberg. The Mountains of the Dragon.'

'The Mountains of the Dragon,' Jenny repeated softly. Her eyes lit up suddenly. 'It does sound tempting, Lynn.'

'Then grasp the opportunity, Jenny.' Lynn put down her cup and crossed to the window. 'Still raining! Can you remember our last summer day? Heavens, this weather is vile! If it weren't for Donald and the baby I would go with Mom myself.' Turning from the window, she asked more softly, 'Why don't you want to go, Jenny?'

'There's the cottage,' Jenny said hesitantly, wondering why she could not make up her mind to go.

'No problem. I'll be in every few days to see to things.'

'And then—there's the estate . . .'

'Donald is winding it up for you. He doesn't need you here, Jenny. He said so. In fact, he thinks the

6

change would be good for you.'

Actually it had been Lynn's husband who had hit on the idea in the first place. 'Jenny was at the office,' he had remarked one evening recently. 'She looked a little peaky, darling. Pale and thin, and so tired. You're not happy about Mother going away on her own. Why not let Jenny go with her?'

'Donald thinks it would be a good idea?' Jenny asked uncertainly.

'We all do. You've had a rough time the last few years, Jenny. Both your parents ill for so long . . . all the nursing and sadness . . . I don't suppose you can remember the last time you went to a party or to the cinema.'

'I didn't want to go,' Jenny said swiftly. 'I didn't miss not having a social life.'

'Of course, I know that.' Lynn came back from the window. 'But now it's time for you to take up the threads of living once more. Have you given any thought to what you'd like to do?'

'I've a few things in mind. I haven't quite decided yet.'

'Well then,' Lynn said enthusiastically, 'what better time than now for a holiday? You'll come back refreshed and energetic, and just brimful with plans and ideas. Don't you see that, Jenny?'

'It certainly sounds nice.' Jenny smiled gratefully at her friend. 'I know I can't go on like this. And a holiday would be wonderful. It's just . . . Oh, I seem to be all mixed up at the moment. When do you want an answer?'

'By tomorrow, if possible.'

7

'I'll sleep on it, then. Another cup of tea, Lynn? And a scone?'

'Just a quick cup. Then I must go.' Lynn glanced at her watch. 'Heavens, look at the time! If I don't get back soon to feed the baby Mom will have a bawling grandchild on her hands.' She began to spread jam on a scone. 'Jenny!' She looked up suddenly, remembering something. 'Do you know, you might even meet a friend if you went out there with Mom. Did I tell you that the Stewarts had met Neil in the Drakensberg?'

'Neil?' Jenny looked puzzled. 'Neil who?'

'Neil who used to live here in the village. Years ago. Don't you remember him?'

'Neil Donaldson?' Jenny sat bolt upright on her cushion. 'Lynn, you *can't* mean Neil Donaldson?'

'Yes.'

'But . . .' There was a dazed expression on Jenny's face. 'I can't believe it. Neil . . . in the Drakensberg . . .'

'I believe he works there.' Lynn was watching her friend's stunned reaction. 'He's a forester, Sandra Stewart said. Jenny, you look as if you'd seen a ghost.'

'It's the way I feel,' Jenny said shakily. 'Neil . . . after all these years! And I'd given up hope of seeing him ever again.'

'He meant so much to you, then?'

'Neil was my childhood,' Jenny said simply. 'He . . . he was like an older brother to me, Lynn, only more so.'

'I never knew that.'

8

'I loved my parents very dearly, but they were so busy running their shop.' Jenny spoke slowly, her eyes soft and distant. 'During the day I hardly saw them. And yet I never minded because I had Neil. He lived next door. And he was the best friend a little girl could have had.'

'He must have been much older than you.'

'Six years.' She paused to consider. 'Neil must be thirty now. It's so hard to believe. Last time I saw him he was a boy, now he's a man. Perhaps he's married and has children of his own. Oh, Lynn, you don't know how often I've wondered what became of him. He always loved the outdoors, but I never dreamed he was a forester, or that he lived so far away.' She glanced at her friend. 'Do you remember him, Lynn?'

'Not really. I hardly knew him, Jenny. I think we came to live here at about the time that he left the village.' Lynn wrinkled her brow. 'Wasn't there some scandal?'

'Yes. It was horrible. His father was involved in a court case. I was so young at the time that I don't think I understood it at all, but I remember how people talked. And Neil was so unhappy. Once he cried, and I was so frightened.'

'Was it then that they left the village?'

'Yes. When the trial was over Neil and his mother moved away. I was so upset, Lynn. I thought I would never get over it.'

'And yet . . . Forgive me, Jenny, but you didn't speak of him often. Until now I'd never realised how much he meant to you.'

9

'I was only ten at the time,' Jenny said thoughtfully. 'And at that age grief passes quickly. There was school, and games. And then you came, Lynn, and we became friends. It's been only recently . . .' Her words trailed away as she got to her feet and went to the window. Lynn watched her, a small slight figure against the background of the never-ceasing rain. 'With all the unhappiness . . .' she was speaking once more, softly, sadly, 'I've been thinking of Neil more and more often.'

Again she was silent, and Lynn thought it best not to question her. It was beginning to grow dark. Jenny had not yet switched on the lights, and only the flickering firelight gave warmth and life to the room. Lynn got to her feet and drew on a coat and scarf. 'You'll let me know whether you'll go?' she asked.

'Of course.' Jenny walked to the door with her. 'Lynn, whatever I decide—thank you for the invitation.' She smiled suddenly. 'You're a good friend.'

When Lynn had gone Jenny went back to the fire. Curling up on the carpet, with her head on the cushion, she stared thoughtfully into the glowing embers. Perhaps Lynn was right, and what she needed was a holiday. Two years ago she had given up her office job to nurse her parents. Now the time had come to step out into the world once more. What better way to begin than by spending three months away from home, basking in sunshine, walking and swimming and climbing.

Perhaps she would find Neil. It was true that he had been in her thoughts more and more often recently. For Neil was the past—not the immediate unhappy

10

past, but the past of her childhood. The carefree happy childhood that seemed so very long ago.

Though Neil had had many friends of his own age, he had always had time to listen to her chatter, to help her when she was in trouble, to take her boating or swimming or walking. ' Jin-Jin,' he would call her when he consoled her after some mishap. ' Dry your tears, Jin-Jin. Everything will be all right.' And with Neil to make it so it always was.

Now her mind was flooded with memories, Neil, teaching her to swim, holding her chin when she was certain she would swallow water. Neil, taking a splinter out of her foot when she had balanced barefoot on a log fence. Neil, fighting a boy who had tried to hurt her, emerging from the fray with a bleeding nose and glowing eyes.

Neil! Neil who was the only link with the past now that her parents had died.

She rose and went to the window. It was still raining, a soft seeping rain that seemed never-ending. Straining her eyes she peered out into the gathering darkness. A cluster of roses had come loose from a trellis and hung drooping and sodden. A cat slunk through the garden, jumped over the wall and vanished. All at once the feeling of bleak desolation was more than she could bear.

A vision swam before her eyes—mountains and forests bathed in sunshine, and Neil waiting to welcome her. By the time she turned from the window to stir up the fire her decision had been made.

Next morning Jenny told her friend that she would

accompany her mother to South Africa. Thereafter things happened quickly. There was so much to do—travel requirements and health regulations to be complied with; clothes to be bought.

Jenny took a long hard look at her wardrobe and decided that the tweeds and jerseys which were so suitable for life in an English village were not the right garments for a holiday in the sun. Early one morning she and Mrs Ramsden, Lynn's mother, travelled to London and spent a glorious day shopping. Lynn was waiting for them when they got back, and enthused over the things Jenny had bought—cotton dresses in vivid colours, slacks and blouses, two skirts for the evening, and a pair of multi-coloured sandals.

The days passed in such a buzz of activity that at night Jenny fell into bed exhausted. Even the plane trip to South Africa and the subsequent train journey passed in a kind of dream. A hotel car was waiting for them at the station, and then at last they were on the last stage of their journey.

When they left the station Jenny looked around her, expecting to find mountains towering above her. But she was disappointed, for all she could see was a line of peaks on the horizon, so far away that they were insubstantial and without form, almost like clouds.

But the further they drove, the more rolling became the countryside. Soon they were entering the foothills of the Drakensberg. With growing fascination Jenny watched the undulating landscape unfolding on either side of her. It was a pretty landscape, rolling and gentle. Sheep cropped at the sparse grass and there were fields with tall, unfamiliar crops. Once the car had to stop and wait while a herd of cows moved from one side of the road to the other.

Higher climbed the car, and higher, and now the ephemeral line of peaks came closer, grew taller, began to acquire shape and form.

Presently the driver turned and smiled. 'When we get round that bend you'll see the hotel,' he said.

Excitedly Jenny sat forward in her seat. Then they were past the bend, and there it was, a small cluster of buildings nestling in a clump of pines. A spiral of smoke rose above the trees, giving the hotel a homely, welcoming appearance. Mrs Ramsden looked at Jenny and smiled.

The formalities over, Jenny and Mrs Ramsden were shown to their bungalow, thatched and round and whitewashed, with a vivid red creeper climbing its walls. Inside, the bungalow was just as pretty. Turquoise curtains picked out the colour of the woven bedspreads and carpets, and though the room was simple it had an inviting warmth and appeal. Jenny ran to the window, opened it wide, and saw they had a splendid view of the mountains. 'It's beautiful!' she cried impulsively. Then, turning back into the room, she saw that Mrs Ramsden looked tired.

'Shall I order tea and some sandwiches?' she suggested. 'I'll unpack for us both, and you could have a rest.'

'I'd like that,' said Mrs Ramsden gratefully. 'The journey tired me more than I had thought it would.'

'You'll feel better after you've had a rest.'

'I'm sure I will. And while I'm resting, you *will*

go and explore, won't you, Jenny?'

'If you're certain you won't be needing me.'

'All I need right now is a good sleep. Jenny,' there was a look of concern in the warm brown eyes. 'My dear, I want you to enjoy yourself while we're here.'

'Oh, but I will,' the girl said eagerly. 'It's all so beautiful—the little I've seen of it.'

'I don't want you to feel that you must spend your time with me. You're young, and I'm old, and the two generations have different needs.'

'I came to be with you,' Jenny said quietly.

'Only as a friend, and to help me when I need it. But I'm neither ancient nor bedridden, my dear. I'll be perfectly happy spending my time in this lovely garden, with the sun warming my bones, while I knit for Lynn's precious baby. Perhaps I'll even find people of my age to be friends with. I'd enjoy the odd natter. But that's not for you. I want you to get out, make friends, go exploring.' She smiled suddenly. 'I must be able to write to Lynn that your cheeks have colour and your eyes the glow of the Jenny we used to know.'

'You're a darling, Mrs Ramsden.' Jenny stretched out a hand to the older woman. 'You and Lynn . . . And I *will* enjoy myself, I promise.'

'Rose said something about Neil Donaldson.' Mrs Ramsden watched as Jenny opened a suitcase and began to hang up dresses.

'Yes. Apparently he's a forester.'

'I hardly knew him,' Mrs Ramsden said thoughtfully. 'But you were friendly with him, weren't you?'

'Very.' Jenny wondered how much Lynn had told

her mother. 'It's hard to believe Neil is here. I've wondered so often what became of him.'

'You'll try to find him?'

'Yes.' Jenny turned from the cupboard. 'It's what I want more than anything else. I think . . . Oh, was that a knock? It must be the tea.'

Mrs Ramsden was very tired. They had their tea in silence, and Neil was not mentioned again. When they had finished Jenny helped Mrs Ramsden to lie down, and covered her with a rug. Then she changed out of her travelling clothes, put on a blouse and a pair of slacks, and closing the door softly behind her she went out into the garden.

On arrival at the hotel there had been little time for more than just a very quick impression of their surroundings. Now Jenny walked slowly through the gardens, enjoying the beauty all around her; the lush green lawns, the big spreading trees, shrubs and bushes bright with exotic flowers.

Finding a wooded path that led away from the hotel she decided to explore. Twigs crackled underfoot and there was the sound of rushing water. Suddenly she was out of the trees and at a stream. She walked a little way along the stony bank, enjoying the crunch of the pebbles beneath her feet. Then, seeing an enormous rock, sheltered and invitingly curved, she sat down and leaned back.

Jenny drew deep breaths of the mountain air. How crisp and fresh it was! She felt, all at once, as light-headed as if she had just downed a glass of sparkling wine.

It was very still. The buzzing of insects and the

gurgle of the water rushing over the rocks seemed only to enhance the stillness. Above everything towered the mountains, folded one behind the other, tall, rugged, brooding, mysterious. The great escarpment seemed to stretch without end as far as the eye could see. There was something primitive about all this beauty, something basic and real and close to nature. Something, Jenny thought, and knew all at once that she had been right to come here.

She left the rock and slithered over loose pebbles to the water. Kneeling down, she cupped her hands to catch some water. She dashed the water over her face and gasped for breath as the iciness hit her with a shock. The water dried quickly and she felt the sun on her face once more.

She laughed suddenly. It was a lovely laugh, joyous and unexpected. It was the first time she had laughed for a long time. 'I'm going to love it here,' she thought. Tomorrow she would enquire about Neil. Her happiness would be complete when she found him. But for today it was enough to sit here by the clear cold mountain stream, and watch the sun set behind the mountains.

Already the lower slopes were shadowed, though the peaks still shone with the dazzling colours of sunset. At last only the highest peak still glowed, magnificent and majestic. Then the sun dipped out of sight, and even the high peak grew dark.

Jenny picked up a twig and tossed it into the water, watching as it turned upon itself, was dashed against a stone, then was gathered up by the water and hurtled downstream towards some unknown destination. When the twig was gone she got to her feet. With the setting of the sun it had grown chilly, and slowly, happily, she began to make her way back to the hotel.

# CHAPTER TWO

Jenny was up early next morning. A glance at Mrs Ramsden's bed showed her that the older woman was still sleeping. She got out of bed quietly and padded about on bare feet while she dressed. With her shoes in her hands she left the room and closed the door gently behind her.

There was a spring in her step as she walked through the garden. The grass was still wet with dew, and bushes glistened with gossamer webs of moisture. Jenny was glad she had worn a cardigan, for the early morning air was chilly, and yet so crisp and invigorating that she felt exhilarated and ready for anything. She took the path that led to the river, and reaching the water she slithered over the stones again with the abandon of a child.

Mist shrouded the peaks, and only the lower slopes of the mountains were visible, but the morning held the promise of a glorious day.

Presently, in the distance, she heard the dull boom of the breakfast gong, and knew it was time to make her way back. When she knocked at the door of the bungalow she found Mrs Ramsden dressed and ready.

18

'Jenny!' she exclaimed, her eyes lighting with pleasure. 'You look wonderful! Your cheeks are glowing.' She put out a hand to touch Jenny's face. 'And so cold. Have you been swimming?'

'Not so early.' Jenny laughed—laughter was coming easily all at once. 'I went for a walk. Oh, Mrs Ramsden, it's beautiful here. I'm so happy Lynn asked me to come.'

'So am I—for both our sakes. Well, Jenny, I don't know about you, but this mountain air seems to have whetted my appetite. Are you ready for breakfast?'

'More than ready. I'm ravenous!'

When Jenny had finished her third piece of toast and was sipping her final cup of tea, she looked up to find Mrs Ramsden smiling at her. 'Enjoy your breakfast, dear?'

'Oh, yes.' She lowered her cup and said apologetically, 'I guess I made a pig of myself?'

'Not at all. It did me good to watch you. I like to see a young girl enjoying her food.'

'I'll get fat if I go on like this,' the girl said ruefully.

'Not with your build. Besides, it's what your body needs after the hard time you've had.'

'Must be something about the mountain air, as you said.' Jenny took another sip from her cup. 'What shall we do this morning, Mrs Ramsden?'

'I know what I shall do. I saw a bench by a little pool, and all around it were the prettiest flowers. I shall sit there with my knitting and look at the mountains.'

'And I'll bring my sketch-pad. That view would

inspire anybody.'

'Perhaps you could find another view to inspire you, Jenny.' Mrs Ramsden hesitated. 'I wonder if you'd mind very much, dear, if I sat in the garden alone? Do you see that table in the corner? There was a lady sitting there—oh, no, she's gone now—and she had such a sweet face. She kept glancing this way, as if she'd like to be friends.'

'And you think if you were sitting alone she might join you?'

'It's what I was hoping, dear.'

'All right, then.' Jenny grinned, knowing Mrs Ramsden was finding a tactful way of telling her to go out alone and enjoy herself. 'I'll just have to take my sketch-pad elsewhere.'

'Thank you, dear.' And they smiled at each other in perfect understanding.

A little later, when she had seen Mrs Ramsden comfortably settled in the garden, her knitting bag and a tea tray on a small table beside her, Jenny went to the bungalow and fetched her pad and pencils. Then she walked to the office. The receptionist's name was Ann. She was a pretty girl with glossy dark hair and merry eyes. 'Hello, Miss Windham,' she said, looking up from her work. 'Can I help you?'

'Please, I thought I'd go for a walk. But I don't know my way around yet.'

'Of course.' The girl's smile was friendly as she put down her pen. 'There are so many beautiful walks. You must try them all while you're here.'

'I'd like that.'

'There's one in particular—to a little grotto. It's

20

easy walking, and very pretty. Perhaps you would like to try it today? I'll tell you how to get there.'

'Actually,' Jenny said, 'I thought I'd walk in the forests.'

'The forests? They're quite a bit further, and you're not used to that much walking yet.'

'I've a reason for wanting to go to the forests.' Jenny hesitated. Then she decided to confide in Ann. 'I want to find a forester.'

'A forester?' The girl's chin went up and her face took on a defensive expression.

'His name is Neil Donaldson.'

'Neil Donaldson?' The defensive expression had left the other girl's eyes and now she looked merely puzzled. 'Neil Donaldson,' she repeated slowly.

'You don't know him?' Jenny asked.

'I don't think I've heard that name before.'

'Oh . . .' Jenny bit her lip. 'I was so certain . . . I'd heard . . . A friend said he'd been seen in these parts.'

'Well, I can't swear to it, of course, but I'd have thought I'd have heard the name if he worked near here,' Ann said. Jenny's disappointment must have been apparent, for she added after a moment, 'Look, Miss Windham, I'll ask around. If I hear of Neil Donaldson, I'll let you know. Now what about this morning? Shall I direct you to the grotto?'

'No,' Jenny said after a moment. 'I would still like to walk in the forests. I've not grown used to this heat yet. I think I'd enjoy walking among the trees.'

She watched as Ann drew a rough map, and listened to the verbal instructions on how to follow it. Then she set out.

21

Behind the hotel Jenny found the path Ann had described, and she began to follow its winding progress up the mountain. Every now and then she stopped to take breath and rest a few moments, for she had had so little exercise in recent months that she found the climb strenuous. But demanding though the walk was, Jenny was enjoying herself.

The track turned and twisted, showing her ever-changing vistas of the mountains. In parts, where the vegetation encroached on the path, she had to push aside the long grass. In other places she walked through soft sand. Once, when she came to a part which was particularly smooth, she sat down and removed her shoes. Then she walked on, enjoying the feel of the soft sand between her toes.

In the distance she could see the green of the forests. But she was to find that distance could be deceptive in the mountains, and it took much longer to reach them than she had imagined.

She came to a stream, and saw that the path continued on the other side. There was no bridge, but boulders had been placed in the water at strategic intervals, forming a kind of natural bridge. Doubtfully Jenny looked at the boulders. They looked slippery and a little dangerous. But she had come so far . . . Once more she took off her shoes and prepared to wade through the stream. Though she knew the water would be cold, the sheer iciness caught at her breath, and she was glad to get to the other side.

At last she came to the forests, and she shivered as she left the sun and walked into the trees. To her surprise she found she was not in a forest as she had imagined it. Rather, this was a jungle of very tall trees, thin and gnarled and intertwining with one another in their struggle to reach the sun. There were trees with roots above the ground, and with gnarled growths knotted and coiled about them. There were moss-covered rocks, and strange exotic flowers, and all about there was the pervading smell of rotting vegetation.

Jenny's first impulse was to stop and go back. Obviously she had taken the wrong path and had got lost. This was not the type of forest she had meant when she had spoken to the hotel receptionist. Then she saw that she was still on a path. A path must lead somewhere, she reasoned, and a sudden feeling of adventure overcame her. What did it matter that this was not what she had expected? She was in a strange country, and on holiday. She would go further.

She heard the sound of rushing water, and at a bend in the path she came to a waterfall. The water tumbled over sheer rocks into a big pool. The pool was dark and silent, a goblin's pool, probably bottomless, Jenny imagined. Cupping her hands, she lifted a little water to wet her hot face, then she sat on a rock and looked about her. It was very quiet in the jungle, and she had the feeling there was not another living being within miles. After a while she walked further, following the path as it twisted and turned through the undergrowth.

As suddenly as she had entered the jungle she was out of it once more. With a lifting of the heart she looked about her. Now she really was in a forest—a forest of tall straight trees, planted in orderly lines. A man-made forest. Where a forest was planted by man it must be cared for by men. Perhaps she would find someone who knew of Neil and could tell her of his whereabouts.

Further she walked into the forest, and further, taking deep breaths of the spicy resinous aroma, and enjoying the smoothness of the pine needles beneath her feet. Presently she came to a clearing. Logs were stacked in neat bundles, and broken twigs were scattered where trees had been felled—clear signs of foresting activity.

Jenny was tired after her long walk. She sat down on the pine needles and leaned back against a pile of logs. It was pretty in the clearing. The sun slanted down through the trees, throwing patterns of dancing light on the forest floor, and there was an air of calm and rusticity which Jenny found very soothing. After a while she took her sketch-pad and pencils from the pocket of her slacks, and began to draw. She became so absorbed in what she was doing that she could not have said afterwards which she became aware of first—the dog rushing towards her, or the voice of the man who said, ' Not bad at all.'

' Oh!' She sat up with a startled exclamation. ' You gave me a fright!'

A man stood beside her, one hand resting reassuringly on the neck of his dog. He was a tall man, lithe and muscular in his neat safari suit, and she thought he must be middle-aged, for his hair was greying at the temples. Then, as he turned his face slightly, her heart gave a lurch at the sight of the scar that raked savagely down his right cheek.

'I'm sorry I frightened you,' he was saying. 'I didn't mean to. I just . . .' The words trailed away and an odd expression came into his eyes.

'It wasn't your fault.' She smiled suddenly. 'I suppose I was just so absorbed in my sketching that I didn't hear you.'

'You've caught the atmosphere well.' He was looking thoughtfully down at her paper. 'Are you here on holiday?'

'Yes. All the way from England.'

'I can hear that by your speech. It's a long way to come.'

'It's a very long holiday. Three months, actually. I'm here as a companion to a lady who's been ill—though she doesn't seem at all weak since we've been here. In fact, she was very keen that I should go exploring by myself.' It was odd, Jenny thought, how she was pouring out words to this man. Though at first she had thought him middle-aged, his voice revealed that he was much younger than she had imagined.

'I see,' he said. 'Well, it's a beautiful place to come to recuperate. You must enjoy walking to have come so far.'

'I wouldn't have undertaken it if I hadn't had a special reason. You see, I'm looking for someone—a forester. I thought I might find him here.'

'Really?' said the man, after a long moment. 'I'm the forester here. My name is Ross Sundy.'

'And I'm Jenny Windham. Mr Sundy,' she looked

at him eagerly, 'perhaps you can help me. I'm looking for a man called Neil Donaldson.'

'Oh?'

'Yes. He's a boy I grew up with. We lost touch—oh, ages ago.'

'And what made you think you'd find him here?'

'I heard that someone had met him.'

'And you came all this way to find him?'

'It certainly helped sway my decision when Mrs Ramsden's daughter asked me to accompany her mother. Neil and I . . . well, we were very close.' She laughed softly. 'He even said sometimes that he would marry me when I grew up.'

'And you've come all this way to remind him of his promise.' A mocking tone had crept into his voice. 'All the way from England to marry a man you've not seen since you were a child?'

'You're being unnecessarily nasty, aren't you?' she said, trying to keep her voice steady. 'But then you wouldn't understand. My parents died, both after a long illness. Neil . . . Neil is my only link with the past. I loved Neil. I'd do all I can to find him.'

'He isn't here, Miss Windham,' the forester said.

'But my friend . . . she was so certain . . . she'd met some friends in London, Les and Sandra Stewart. They'd been here and seen him.'

'Perhaps they were mistaken,' said Ross Sundy. 'Perhaps they saw him elsewhere, and got confused. Or your friend used the name of this man as bait to get you to accompany her mother.'

'No!' cried Jenny violently. 'Lynn would never be so cruel! She knows how much Neil meant to me.

26

I can't believe she'd do a thing like that to me.'

'Well then, isn't it possible that . . .' His voice trailed away. 'I'm afraid I can't solve this for you, Miss Windham. But I have a cottage not far from here. Will you come and have a cup of coffee with me there?' When she looked at him suspiciously, doubting his sudden friendliness, he added, 'I really didn't mean to upset you. Will you come?'

'All right,' she said, after a moment. Perhaps she had misjudged the man, she thought. Perhaps he had not meant to sound quite so mocking just now, or perhaps it really did seem strange that a girl would remember an attachment from so long ago. In any event, she was tired and thirsty, and it might seem ungrateful to refuse his invitation.

When they came to his cottage she offered to make the coffee, but he told her to sit down and make herself comfortable. Curiously she looked about her. The cottage was not big, but from where she sat it was difficult to tell how many rooms it comprised. The room where she waited seemed to double as sitting-room and office. In one corner was a table, with a few comfortable chairs surrounding it. Maps hung on the walls and near the door was a big filing cabinet. The room was clean and neat and very functional—too functional, perhaps, for something was missing. For a moment she could not put a finger on it. Was it that there was nothing in this room that did not serve its purpose? Nothing that seemed personal, that held a clue to the personality of the man who lived here? Jenny had the feeling that if Ross Sundy were to move on, he would leave no imprint of himself on the place where he had lived.

'Shall we have it outside?' The forester had returned to her, carrying a tray. There were two cups of coffee and a plate of bread, sliced and spread with butter and jam.

'Thanks, I'd love that,' she said. Near the cottage beneath some tall trees stood a rustic wooden table and two chairs. 'I feel as if I could get drunk on all this beauty,' Jenny observed when she had sat down. 'I just can't seem to get my fill of it.'

'You don't think you'll be longing for England by the time your three months here are over?'

The smile left Jenny's eyes and she was silent as she thought of her home in the village, empty now, and so lonely. A lump came into her throat, so hard that she could not have spoken.

'You're not still thinking of Neil Donaldson?' Ross Sundy asked after some time. 'Hoping he'll pitch up and marry you? Then you wouldn't have to go back.'

'You . . . !' She sprang to her feet and turned blindly from him. The quicker she got away from this arrogant man the better.

'Miss Windham . . .' He put out a hand and grasped her wrist. 'Don't go.'

'Leave go of my hand!' She was even more vehement now, for the touch of his hand on her skin was unexpectedly tingling.

'Then will you sit down again and finish your coffee?' His voice was softer now, and more gentle. 'This is the second time I've upset you. I'm sorry. There—that's better. Now take a deep breath and

28

count to ten, then by the time you've finished counting you won't feel like hurling your cup at my head.'

In spite of herself she had to laugh. His face was so very serious, only the twinkle in his eyes betraying his teasing. 'All right,' she said at last. 'If only because this is such a nice cup and I wouldn't like to break it.'

'I suppose I shouldn't question your priorities. My head being less important than the cup. Let's just say as long as you don't throw it—that's all that matters.'

'You're quite impossible,' Jenny said.

'Absolutely,' he agreed cheerfully, and then they were both laughing, and the tension between them had crumbled.

'The ogre of the forest, that's me,' said Ross Sundy. 'Be careful, Miss Windham, you might not get out of here alive.'

'I'm scared stiff.' Again she was laughing. He was so much nicer now that the mocking tone had vanished.

'Do you always eat so much when you're scared stiff?' he asked with a twinkle, as she took another slice of bread.

'It's only my third piece.'

'Fourth."

'Fourth, then.' She sighed. 'Do you know, I've developed the most ravenous appetite since we've been in the mountains. Where it's to end I don't know. Perhaps I'll turn into a mountain myself. Then I won't be able to walk any more, and I'll just have to stay put.'

'And there will be a new mountain called the Jenny Windham. Somehow '—he glanced at her so thoughtfully that an unexpected thrill slid down the nerves of her spine—' I should think there's little possibility of that happening, little Miss Windham. Ah, finished already? Do have another.'

'Definitely not.' She laughed. 'I must stop somewhere.' She looked at her watch. 'Good heavens— the time! Mrs Ramsden will be sending a search party out to look for me.' She got to her feet. 'Thanks for the coffee, Mr Sundy. I think I must be going now.'

'I'll walk back with you. There's something I need from the hotel store,' said Ross Sundy. 'Now will be as good a time as any to get it.'

'Oh, that will be nice.' Her formal words hid her delight, for much as she had enjoyed herself in the forest, she knew that she would enjoy the walk back even more. As Ross Sundy closed the door of his cottage, she said, 'Mr Sundy, if you hear anything about Neil Donaldson, will you tell me?'

He turned. She thought there was a wary look in his eyes. 'I won't be hearing.'

'How can you be so sure?' she asked uncertainly.

'Because, Miss Windham, I know the names of all the foresters around here,' he told her, and now the closed look had spread over the whole of his face. 'If there were anyone by that name anywhere in the area, I would know.'

'But . . .' She started to speak, then stopped, sensing the futility of it.

30

'This way,' he said, and they began to follow the path through the forest. For the first few minutes they walked in silence, but gradually the strain began to vanish from his face, and he began to talk. He pointed out different trees to her, told her about the forest, about the jungle too, and how the two came to be so close to each other. Once a brightly coloured bird flew from a tree with a great clattering of wings, and he told her its name and a little about its habits. Only Neil's name was never mentioned, and Jenny made up her mind not to bring it up again.

When they came to the stream Ross Sundy leapt quickly across the boulders, nimble as a mountain goat. Then he looked back at Jenny and saw her studying the slippery stones with trepidation. She would wade through the water, of course—just as she had done on the way up. She was just deciding on the best course.

'You need help,' Ross Sundy called. With a few quick steps he was back and holding his hand out to her. With Ross's help Jenny found it easy to step from boulder to boulder. This time there were no half-way stops in the icy water. Neil used to help her like this. She remembered how he would ease her way over stiles and fences.

But her skin had never tingled at Neil's touch. This, she knew all at once, was the difference between Ross Sundy and Neil Donaldson.

All too soon they reached the path that led to the hotel, and here Ross Sundy said goodbye to her, for the way to the store was along a different road. 'Be seeing you,' he said, raised a hand in farewell, then smiled and went on his way.

Jenny stool still for a long moment, watching the tall lithe figure walk away from her. Then she too walked further.

# CHAPTER THREE

'Did you find your way to the forest?' Jenny was walking past the office when the receptionist called to her.

'Yes, thanks.' Jenny stopped and smiled at Ann. 'Your directions were very easy to follow.'

'I'm glad.'

'Of course, I didn't expect anything like the jungle. It was quite an eerie feeling when I first found myself in it.'

'I suppose it would be,' Ann laughed. 'It's quite a shock when you've never been in one before. I suppose I should have warned you, but I didn't think of it. Incidentally, you didn't come across the man you mentioned . . . ? What was his name—Neville?'

'Neil. Neil Donaldson. No, I didn't meet him, but I met another forester.'

'You did?' Ann glanced at her sharply.

'Ross Sundy. Do you know him?'

'Yes.'

'He invited me to have a cup of coffee with him at his cottage.'

'You had coffee with Ross?' All at once the light left the other girl's eyes and her tone became hostile.

'Was there anything wrong in that?' Jenny asked, a little taken aback by the change in the girl's attitude.

'I suppose not. But I must admit I'm a little surprised.'

'Why?'

'Ross doesn't usually ask strangers to his cottage.'

'Well, perhaps it was just the circumstances of our meeting,' Jenny said lightly.

'Oh?'

'I wasn't far from his cottage when he came across me. We got talking about Neil, and Mr Sundy was rather rude. Perhaps he felt he had to treat me to coffee as an apology.'

'I see.' The other girl did not look altogether appeased. 'And did Ross know of Neil Donaldson?'

'He said he'd never heard of him,' Jenny said, after a moment.

'Then you can be sure he doesn't operate around here.'

'Perhaps not,' Jenny said quietly, and taking leave of Ann she went on her way.

'Hello, dear.' Mrs Ramsden was in the garden where Jenny had left her earlier that morning. 'Have a good day?'

'Lovely, thanks. And you?'

'Oh, yes, indeed.' Happily she told Jenny about her new friend. 'The lady I hoped would join me did so. She's here with her son, but he was out climbing. We had such a nice morning, Jenny. Especially as we found we had a lot in common.'

'I'm glad you've made a friend.' Jenny leaned wearily back in her chair. 'Now if, I go off on my own I won't feel that I'm neglecting you.'

'You don't neglect me. Well, Jenny, what did you do?'

'I went into the forest.'

'Oh?' Mrs Ramsden's gaze was instantly alert. 'You went after your friend?'

'Yes.'

'Was he glad to see you?'

'He wasn't there.'

'Never mind,' Mrs Ramsden said comfortingly. 'Perhaps he was busy with his duties in some other part of the forest. You're sure to meet up with him sooner or later, Jenny. After all, we're going to be here for some time.'

'No.' Jenny's eyes were troubled. 'You don't understand, Mrs Ramsden. He isn't here. He doesn't seem to be in these forests.'

'Oh, Jenny, I'm sorry.' The older woman's eyes were full of concern. 'I know how much you were looking forward to seeing him again.'

'And yet Lynn said he'd been seen here,' Jenny mused.

'Perhaps Lynn made a mistake,' her mother said slowly.

'No, Lynn doesn't make mistakes like that.'

'Or perhaps he's been transferred to another district,' Mrs Ramsden suggested.

'Perhaps.' Jenny was quiet for a moment. 'It's just . . . Mrs Ramsden, I have the oddest feeling something is wrong.'

'Nonsense, dear. Just because Lynn got her facts a little mixed . . .'

'I don't think she did. Mrs Ramsden, do you know, I met another forester, a man called Ross Sundy. I asked him about Neil, and he said he'd never seen him, never even heard about him.'

'Perhaps he hasn't,' said Mrs Ramsden reasonably.

'I'd agree with you if it weren't for the look in his eyes when he spoke.'

'What do you mean, Jenny?' Now Mrs Ramsden was curious. 'What kind of look?'

'I wish I could describe it. He looked defensive . . . wary . . . as if he was on his guard. He was so sarcastic too. And yet all this was only when we spoke about Neil.'

'You talked about other things too, then?'

'Yes. In fact, we had coffee at his cottage and he was perfectly charming.'

'Jenny, you're quite certain you're not imagining any of this?'

'No, I'm almost certain I'm not.'

'Jenny dear, perhaps I shouldn't say this . . .' the older woman was choosing her words carefully, 'but you do know how much I care for you, and so I know you won't be offended . . .'

'What is it?' Jenny asked quietly.

'Well, dear, I know how much you'd been banking on seeing your friend again. Lynn told me about Neil, and how you had lost touch with him, how he was your link with the past. You've had a hard time, Jenny.' She looked up at the girl's rapt face, and then bent her head over her knitting. Jenny thought she had decided not to go on with what she was saying, but after a moment she continued, 'Jenny, do you think it's possible that you've been wanting to see Neil so much that . . . that . . .'

'That I imagine defensiveness and wariness because a man tells me he's never heard of him?' Jenny felt tears pricking at her eyelids. So even Mrs Ramsden did not believe her when she said there was something amiss.

'Jenny . . . Jenny, please don't upset yourself so much. I didn't mean to suggest . . .'

'It's all right.' The girl forced a smile. 'You think I've developed an obsession about Neil. Well, perhaps I have.'

'No, not an obsession. Jenny, isn't it possible that the Stewarts meant a different part of the country? After all, the Drakensberg is such a very long range of mountains.'

'It *is* possible.' Jenny changed the subject. 'Anyway, I'm glad you made a friend. What's her name?'

'Mrs Langley. As I was telling you, Mrs Langley has a son. He's a mountaineer. He's training for some tremendous climb.'

'Where will he be climbing?' Jenny asked without very much interest.

'His mother did tell me, but I just can't think of the place at this moment. That's something you'll be able to ask him yourself. Mrs Langley wants to introduce him to you.'

'Perhaps one day,' Jenny murmured.

'I think—they may join us in the lounge after dinner this evening,' Mrs Ramsden told her.

'Golly, Mrs Ramsden!' Jenny's eyes were twinkling. 'It sounds as if you two ladies are trying your hands at a little matchmaking.'

'Jenny!' Mrs Ramsden's cheeks reddened so swiftly that the girl knew her jest had come close to the truth. 'Who said anything about matchmaking? But you're a young girl, and he's a young man, and you're both alone. Why shouldn't you be friends while we're here?'

'I was teasing. In any event, if Mrs Langley's son is training for a climb he's not likely to be interested in me.' Jenny began to gather up her friend's belongings. 'I think I hear the gong calling us to lunch.'

'And you're hungry, of course.'

'Of course. Ravenous!' And Jenny laughed as they walked up to the hotel together.

Though Neil's name was not mentioned again that day he continued to remain in Jenny's thoughts. In the late afternoon she went again to the river. As she watched the sun begin to set behind the mountain peaks she relived the events of the morning.

She knew she had not imagined the wariness in Ross Sundy's eyes. Though he had masked the expression almost immediately, it had lurked in his eyes long enough for her to see it. It was an expression which Jenny could not exactly define, nor could she tell precisely what it meant. But she did not believe Ross Sundy was telling the truth when he said he had never heard of Neil. Yet why? Why was he so adamant about his denial?

Jenny's eyes searched the mountains, resting on

the forested slopes in the distance. Lynn wasn't wrong, I'm not wrong, she thought, why all this mystery? Oh, Neil, let there be nothing the matter.

Almost involuntarily, her thoughts slipped to Ross Sundy. Despite her conviction that he was keeping something from her, there was nevertheless something about him that called to every nerve in her body. Just the touch of his hand had been enough to send shivers rushing along her spine. It was a feeling she had never experienced before, and one which she would have liked to banish from her consciousness.

And what of Ann, the receptionist? Whatever else she might have imagined, Jenny knew she had not imagined the girl's hostility when she heard that Jenny had been with Ross Sundy at his cottage. Was Ann interested in Ross? How did he feel about her? Jenny had a mental vision of the other girl, the glossy dark hair, the sparkling brown eyes and the perfectly shaped oval face. What chance would she have against beauty of this kind?

Moodily Jenny watched the dazzling colours of the sunset. She was filled with a vague and gnawing feeling of restlessness, and though she did not care to admit it to herself, she knew the cause of that feeling. There was much more to it than the almost certain knowledge that Neil had been in these mountains, and that Ross Sundy, for reasons of his own, did not want her to know it. It was Ross, the man himself, who had made her feel so uncertain. It was incredible, Jenny thought, that she could have been so affected by him.

After all, she told herself, she was not a child.

She had had boy-friends before this, and none of them had left her weak-kneed and restless. It was ridiculous that Ross, a forester whom she would never see again after her return to England, should be the one to make her feel so strange. She tried to tell herself it was the mountain air, the strange new setting, the delight of being on holiday, that had made her so susceptible to him. And she knew she was not convinced.

Of a sudden the complications the day had brought made her impatient. The sun had left the highest peak in a spurt of glory, and it was beginning to grow chilly. Jenny got to her feet, picked up a stone and hurled it angrily into the water. Then, having given vent to her feelings, she made her way to the hotel.

Later that evening, when dinner was over, Mrs Ramsden and Jenny took their coffee into the lounge. Hot as it had been during the day, when the sun left the mountains the air could grow very cold. In the open brick fireplace a fire crackled and glowed. The burning logs were from trees that grew in the forests, and the fragrance they gave off was sweet-smelling and resinous. The room was cosy, with low timbered ceilings and comfortable chairs set in various places, so that the guests could be sociable or secluded, as they wished. It was both rustic and pretty, and Jenny thought that much care must have gone into achieving the combination.

When she had finished her coffee, Jenny picked up a magazine that lay on a table near her. She had just started to look through the pages, searching for an article that would hold her attention, when she heard Mrs Ramsden say, 'How nice! Yes, please do join us,' and as Jenny looked up an elderly woman and a young man sat down.

'This is my young friend Jenny Windham,' Mrs Ramsden was saying as she made the introductions. 'Jenny dear, I want you to meet Mrs Langley. And this'—she turned to the young man—'must be your son, Mrs Langley?'

'Yes, indeed. I was about to introduce him.' Mrs Langley had merry eyes in an apple-cheeked face, and Jenny, liking her instantly, knew that she and Mrs Ramsden would be firm friends. 'This is my son Andrew. Don't you think Miss Windham is pretty, Andrew?'

'Heavens . . .' Jenny began, taken aback at the unexpectedly direct approach, but Andrew stopped her in mid-sentence.

'Very pretty,' he agreed. He had been taking in the violet eyes under the long gold-tipped lashes, and now he was smiling in open appreciation. 'Mother, I think it would be a good idea if we changed places. I know you want to talk to Mrs Ramsden. And I would like to get to know Miss Windham better.'

'I don't think she'd mind if you called her Jenny—would you, dear?' said Mrs Ramsden, and once again Jenny was astonished at the speed with which things were progressing.

'I'd much prefer it,' Jenny said, and Andrew grinned and said, 'Thank you, Mrs Ramsden. I prefer informality myself. Jenny, I'm Andrew.'

41

Within minutes the two elderly ladies were deep in a discussion about their grandchildren—not, Jenny thought with amusement, as if they had been discussing this very subject most of the morning. Turning to Andrew, she found his twinkling eyes upon her. 'Terrific, aren't they?' he said in a conspiratorial whisper. 'Their grandchildren, bless them, will provide a never-ending and ever-interesting topic for the next few months.'

'You're not a father, are you?' Jenny asked disbelievingly.

'Jeepers, no!' He pulled a face in mock terror. 'I'm not even married. Never yet found the girl who'd put up with me.'

Looking at him, at the open face and merry eyes so much like his mother's, Jenny guessed that it was rather that Andrew had not yet found the girl he wanted to spend his life with.

'No,' he went on, 'the grandchildren are my sister's two, a girl and a boy. Mom dotes on them. She'll miss them while we're here.'

'You said "months" a moment ago . . .'

'That's right. I'm in training for an expedition in the Himalayas later in the year,' Andrew explained. 'I broke a leg a few months ago and couldn't climb for quite a while. Now I must get back into training. Actually, I'm lucky.' He grinned, running his fingers through his dark waving hair. 'I work for a firm that specialises in mountaineering equipment, and my climbing is a good advertisement for them. That's how I managed to get away for so long.'

'And your mother? She doesn't climb, too, surely?'

'Can you imagine it?' he grinned. 'No, but she has some notion that she should see that I eat properly while I'm in training. What she'll do when I'm far away and she can't watch over me I don't know. Still . . .' he glanced affectionately at his mother, 'she means well, and I'm glad she can have a holiday. It's just that she forgets sometimes that I'm a grown man.'

'Mothers are notorious for that sort of thing, aren't they?' Jenny laughed. 'I like her, Andrew.'

'Yes, she's grand.' He looked curiously at Jenny. 'Enough about my mother. What about you people? Mom said you were planning to be here some time too.'

'Mrs Ramsden hasn't been well,' Jenny explained. 'We're from England, and the constant rain hasn't been good for her. Her doctor suggested that she should try to get away for a while, and Lynn, her daughter, hit upon the idea of a holiday here in the mountains.'

'I see. But where do you fit into the pattern, Jenny?' He paused. 'I'm sorry, that's a personal question. Perhaps I shouldn't have asked?'

'Not at all,' Jenny smiled. Andrew was so warm and open that it was hard to imagine taking offence at anything he might say. 'My parents died recently. Lynn seemed to think I needed a holiday too.' She paused, her fingers playing with the fringes of the antimacassar which lay on the arm of her chair. 'Lynn is a good friend. She said she wanted me to accompany her mother because she needed a companion, but personally, I think she was just trying to help me.'

'Well, whatever the reason, I'm delighted you're here.' Andrew delved about in his pocket, drew out a pipe, and began to fill it with tobacco. When he had finished tamping it down he looked at Jenny and smiled. 'I was rather dreading the evenings. My days are busy, but the evenings can be a little boring. Mom is a good old thing, but I was hoping for some young female company. Anyone as pretty as you is really more than I dreamed of finding.'

'You're flattering me,' Jenny laughed. Andrew did not set her pulses racing as Ross Sundy had done, but it was so long since a man had been attentive to her that she enjoyed his compliments, even though she did not take them seriously.

'No, I mean every word.' He had finished lighting his pipe, and drew on it contentedly. 'We'll have fun together, Jenny. During the day I won't be able to see much of you. I spend most of my days climbing—I really am quite serious about getting fit again. But we can be together in the evenings.'

'Does the hotel provide entertainment?' she asked.

'Sometimes. We're so far from the nearest town that it's quite a necessity.'

'Mainly films, I imagine?' Jenny thought that the films shown here might be old ones that she had seen in England years ago, and knew that it would not matter.

'Films—yes. And the occasional bingo evenings. Every now and then there's a dance—nothing grand, but good fun—if you have someone nice to dance with. Which I do have now,' he added grinning.

' Flattering me again!'

' No, really. It will be nice to have you here, Jenny. We won't even be dependent on planned entertainment. Evenings when it's warm we can walk beneath the trees, and the rest of the time we'll sit by the fire and talk.'

' I want to hear about your climbing,' Jenny said. ' If you're planning an expedition in the Himalayas you must be quite an expert.'

' Oh, I'll tell you all about it. I love talking about mountains—you'll probably get so bored that you'll plead with me to stop.'

' I think it's unlikely that I shall. Look, Andrew, the ladies are beginning to look tired. I think I should take Mrs Ramsden to the bungalow.'

' Fine. See you tomorrow then, Jenny. Enjoy your day.'

' And I hope you have a good day's climbing.'

Jenny was still smiling as she and Mrs Ramsden made their way out of the lounge and to their bungalow. It was cold walking through the dark garden, but the air was bracing and fresh, and realising that it would be cold they had brought coats with them. The night was filled with the never-ceasing song of the crickets—the sound of Africa at night, Jenny was to discover—and over-head the sky was clear and studded with thousands of stars. She drew her coat more tightly about her, but if she had not been concerned about Mrs Ramsden she would have lingered a little longer in the garden, enjoying the rustic peace of the mountains at night.

'Would you like me to brush your hair for you?' Jenny asked Mrs Ramsden when she had switched on the light in the bungalow, and turned back the bedspreads.

'Would you, Jenny?'

'Of course.'

'This is nice.' The older woman sighed contentedly as Jenny, having unpinned the long coiled hair, began to brush with smooth, careful strokes. 'So relaxing. You have gentle hands, Jenny. I know I shall sleep well after this.'

'I'm glad. It's what I want to do.'

They were silent a few minutes while Jenny brushed the long hair, soft and glossy still despite its greyness. Then Mrs Ramsden asked, 'What did you think of Andrew, Jenny?'

'He's nice, isn't he?' Jenny said warmly. 'I liked him.'

'I liked him too.' Mrs Ramsden caught the girl's eyes in the mirror. 'You'll have lots of time to get to know each other. Andrew and his mother will be here almost as long as we will.'

'So he was telling me.' If the expression in Mrs Ramsden's eyes meant something, Jenny did not intend rising to it just yet.

'He's almost thirty, you know. His mother was telling me how she wished he'd settle down and get married.'

There were some statements which could not, after all, be ignored. 'Mrs Ramsden,' Jenny stopped brushing and looked at her suspiciously, 'you said earlier that you weren't matchmaking.'

'Well, of course I'm not, dear.' Now the older woman's cheeks in the mirror were flushed, her eyes wide open and innocent. 'I was just telling you what Andrew's mother said.'

'I see.' Jenny resumed the gentle strokes.

'He seems such a nice young man, Jenny, and I believe he's a very capable engineer. It's only now and then that he goes on mountaineering expeditions. In fact, this holiday is just a special training period his firm has given him.'

'Yes, I know.'

'Jenny . . .' Mrs Ramsden turned and looked at her anxiously, 'I haven't said anything out of place, have I?'

'Of course you haven't.' The girl smiled at her reassuringly.

'It's just that . . . well, he does seem such a nice young man. And I can see he comes from a good family. Mrs Langley is an extremely nice woman. And . . . and . . .' She paused, as if she could not quite decide to say what was on her mind.

'You want me to spend time with Andrew?' Jenny queried, helping her out.

Still Mrs Ramsden hesitated. Jenny sensed she was not certain how her words would be received. At last she said, 'I love having you with me, Jenny. It's made all the difference to my holiday. But you are twenty-four, dear, and so much of your life has been duty. I want to see you happy.'

'I *am* happy,' Jenny assured her.

'You think you are. Jenny, you must forgive me for talking like this to you. I wouldn't be saying

47

these things if I weren't so fond of you. My dear, I'm not the right companion for you.'

'Lynn thought I was,' Jenny said quietly.

'For a holiday like this, yes, just in case I need help of some kind. But that's all. You should be meeting young people, young men—there, I've said it!' She began to twist the rings on her fingers. 'You'd make some man a wonderful wife. And Andrew . . .'

'Andrew is a very nice person,' Jenny said quietly. 'I told you I liked him. But I hardly know him.'

'I know. And it needn't be Andrew. If you find . . . But you'll give yourself a chance, won't you?' Mrs Ramsden begged pleadingly.

'I'll give myself a chance,' Jenny agreed after a long moment. 'I know you have my interests at heart, and I love you for it. But . . . well, when I get married I want to be certain. I don't want to find myself forced into something.'

'I would never dream of forcing you,' Mrs Ramsden said quickly. 'You mustn't think that. I was only suggesting . . .'

'I know. Perhaps I'm just very romantic,' Jenny's eyes were soft and distant, 'but I want to be in love with the man I marry. *Real* love.'

'And with Andrew it couldn't be?'

'I don't know. I don't think so.'

'Jenny . . .' Mrs Ramsden's eyes were troubled, 'it's not Neil, is it?'

'Neil?' Jenny exclaimed, astonished.

'You don't have some idea that you're in love with him just because you knew him so long ago

48

when you were a child?'

'Oh, no!'

'That's all right, then.' She looked a little more reassured. 'I know how disappointed you were not to find him. But . . . Jenny, give yourself a chance. Even if you had found Neil he might have turned into a very different man from the boy you once knew.'

'I know that. I'm not in love with a memory. Really I'm not.'

'You're too sensible.' Wisely Mrs Ramsden dropped the subject. Turning from the dressing-table, she put a hand before her mouth and yawned. 'That was nice, Jenny. Thank you, dear. And now I'm going to say goodnight.'

'Goodnight, Mrs Ramsden.' Jenny hugged her briefly. 'Thank you for being so kind. And don't worry about me. It really isn't necessary.'

When Mrs Ramsden was asleep Jenny went to the window. The curtains were parted, and she leaned out of the open window and took deep breaths of the cold fragrant air. It was too dark now to see the mountains, but she could see where they ended, for they were a greater blackness than the sky. Mysterious and forbidding they looked in the darkness, and yet by virtue of their constancy they were also reassuring.

Somewhere on those dark slopes was a cottage, and in it a tall lean man. Did he sleep, she wondered, or was he still awake, reading perhaps, or making plans for the next day's work?

Mrs Ramsden was mistaken if she imagined that

the thought of Neil could prevent Jenny from falling in love with Andrew Langley. She loved Neil, it was true. She loved him as she remembered him, and she loved him for what he represented—for her childhood, and for the happiness which they had shared.

But she was not *in* love with him. You could not be in love with a man you remembered only as a boy. She wanted to clear up the mystery that surrounded him—for that there was a mystery she was almost certain. She wanted to see Neil again, wanted it more than almost anything else. But not because she loved him in the sense that she wanted to marry him.

Jenny knew that her hesitation over Andrew stemmed from quite a different source, and one which she did not feel she could discuss with Mrs Ramsden. She liked Andrew. He was warm and open and fun to be with. But he was not a man who would ever set her pulses racing or make the blood flow faster in her veins.

He was not a man—like Ross Sundy.

# CHAPTER FOUR

For a time Jenny kept away from the forest. Ross Sundy had made such an impact on her that she was reluctant to meet him again too soon. She was definitely not in love with him, she told herself—after all, she had met him only once—but she was a little frightened of the sensations he had managed to kindle in her.

Even if she did happen to meet him she knew she must pretend complete disinterest. There could be no pursuing a relationship with the man. In three months' time she would be returning to England—that was where her life lay. And the life of Ross Sundy was in the forests of the Drakensberg. If their paths crossed it was a transient thing. Her only purpose in speaking to him must be to find out more about Neil, that was all.

And yet the tremendous attraction she felt for him did serve one purpose. It showed her that she was able to be moved deeply by a man; therefore she must wait until she met another man who could stir her emotions before she could get married.

Each morning when Mrs Ramsden was comfortably seated in the garden, Jenny would plan what she would do that day. Sometimes she knew her destination in advance, knew the cave or pool or hill she was heading for. But often she left the hotel with no definite destination in mind. Finding a track, she would follow it, not knowing where it led, just confident that it would lead to somewhere beautiful. And she was seldom disappointed.

There was so much to see, so much to marvel at in the mountains of the Drakensberg. Sometimes the grass was so high that she could hardly see the path, and then she would reach a rise and catch her breath at the vista that stretched before her: the folding line of the escarpment, velvety green on the nearer slops, and ephemerally blue in the distance.

Often as she walked she would hear the sound of running water, and then as the path curved she would come to the river. The path might run alongside the river for a while before curving away from it once more, but now and then it would continue on the other side of the water, so that Jenny would have to take off her shoes and walk over rocks and slippery boulders in order to cross the river.

Now and then she heard a distant barking. At first she took it to be the barking of dogs, but when she asked Andrew about it later, he told her the sounds were made by baboons. Baboons could be dangerous, and though it was unlikely that they would ever come near to her, he warned her to be careful not to antagonise them by teasing them or throwing stones. Once a far-off movement caught her eyes, and she stood quite still, her eyes searching the bush-covered cliffs where the movement had been, not certain what it was that she had seen.

The movement came again. And suddenly she knew what she was seeing. Baboons! Baboons jumping through the trees, swinging from branches, running through the long grass. She heard again the barking that sounded so much like the sound of dogs. She remained in that spot for a long time, watching the cavorting baboons. Never before had she seen wild animals at play in their natural surroundings. It was at moments like these that the little village in Sussex seemed to have existed in another world.

She would see birds, brightly-coloured and exotic, uttering loud cries as they flew across the sky. There was a strange bird which flew very low, almost touching the ground, its long tail seeming to drag it downwards. After Andrew told her it was a widow-bird, Jenny would watch it with amusement, thinking how aptly it had been named, for the long black tail really looked extraordinarily like widow's weeds.

Jenny spent many days in this manner, just wandering where the different paths led her. Sometimes Ann, the receptionist, suggested a new walk to her. Now that Jenny was not spending her time in the forests, she found the other girl friendly once more, and much more helpful.

In the evening there was Andrew. Andrew was fun. He had a large repertoire of mountaineering tales which kept Jenny fascinated. If at times she suspected him of exaggerating or embellishing a story to give it more suspense, this never detracted from her enjoyment. One of the reasons she enjoyed his company so much was because she could relax with him.

Andrew was able to make her laugh. Sometimes when they were sharing a joke together, Jenny would look up and find Mrs Ramsden and Mrs Langley smiling indulgently in their direction, but after the first few times this did not disturb her. She learned to disregard the meaning looks of the two older women, for though she enjoyed Andrew's company she knew there existed between them nothing more than friendship.

A week or so after her first excursion to the forest Jenny finally decided to walk that way again. It was a particularly hot day, and after walking for a while in the scorching sun she began to feel enervated. Longingly she thought of the forest. There it would be cool and pleasant.

Momentarily she thought of Ross Sundy, and as quickly shrugged the thought away. For the chances of seeing him were slender, and she was silly to deny herself the pleasure of resting in the shade on a day like this.

Presently she reached the jungle. So great was the sudden contrast in temperature that she shivered as she entered that strange silent green world. For a moment she thought of turning back, but by the time she reached the waterfall and the goblin's pool she was glad she had come. It was refreshingly cool in this place where the sun never penetrated.

On she walked through the jungle till at last she came to the forest. Here too it was quiet and cool, but the early part of the walk, beneath the hot sun, had sapped all her energy. When she came to a big rock which looked as if it had been placed there just on purpose for weary travellers, she sat down on the thick carpet of pine needles, leaned back and closed her eyes. She meant only to rest a few minutes, but she must have been more tired than she had realised. She did not feel herself fall asleep.

A hand touched her arm, and Jenny sat up in fright. 'Heavens!' she exclaimed, rubbing her eyes. 'You make a habit of startling me!'

'Lucky it was only I that startled you.' Ross Sundy was standing over her. His face was unsmiling, set in stiff, stern lines.

'I didn't mean to fall asleep,' she said uncertainly, wondering why he looked so angry.

'Don't let it happen again. Ever.' Still he looked at her sternly.

'All right,' she said, without understanding the reason for his displeasure, 'I won't. It was just that I was tired. And it was so comfortable . . .'

'Miss Windham,' he said, almost despairingly, 'how can I make you understand that you're not in England? You just can't let yourself fall asleep in these forests, or anywhere else in the veld or the mountains for that matter.'

Together with the sternness there was a look of concern in his eyes that made her heart beat faster. To hide her confusion she said, almost defiantly, 'I've said I won't. But I still don't think what I did was such a crime.'

'Because you don't understand. Miss Windham . . .'

he bent and stretched out a hand to her, 'get up, I'm going to show you what I mean. Quietly now— very quietly.' Holding her hand in his, he led her soundlessly to the other side of the rock against which she had been leaning.

'What . . .?' she began, puzzled, then stopped as he put a hand over her mouth to quieten her.

'There.' He spoke very quietly.

She glanced from his grave eyes at the spot to which he was pointing. 'Do you see it?' he whispered.

'I . . .' The word came out in a muffled gasp. It was just as well that his hand was still over her mouth, for if it had not been she would have screamed. Obviously it was what he had been trying to prevent. She could only look at him in horror. When he was certain that she had herself under control he let his hand drop to his side.

In a cleft at the foot of the rock lay a snake, green and coiled and sinister.

'Oh!' she whispered, and found she was trembling.

He led her away then, swiftly, quietly, but surprisingly gently.

'What is it?' she asked, when she could speak.

'A mamba.'

'Is it—poisonous?'

'Deadly,' he said tersely. 'One of the deadliest snakes in Africa.'

'Oh, no!' she whispered inadequately. She had a mental vision of what might have happened if the snake had taken it into its head to uncoil itself and explore what lay on the other side of the rock. 'I never dreamed . . .'

'I know, Miss Windham. You think I don't know how you feel, but I do. But perhaps you can understand now why I said you can't sleep here.'

'It looks so peaceful . . .' she protested.

'It is.' The dark eyes drew together in a frown. 'But you must be aware of possible dangers. It could have been a scorpion . . . anything.'

'I'll be careful from now on.' Her voice was flat, quite without any expression. She felt absolutely calm, but the calm was tinged with an icy numbness. The shock had not yet hit her.

And then as they walked together beneath the trees a small white butterfly flew past. It came from behind her, fluttering suddenly into her vision. Jenny uttered a sharp cry of fear and jumped backwards. The next moment she had fallen. A small rock lay in the path just behind her, and she had tripped over it.

She looked up and saw in a blur Ross's face bending over her. Then she put her face in her hands and began to cry. It seemed that the fall had been necessary to release the tension that had built up inside her.

She did not know how long she wept. She did not know that Ross knelt down beside her, but when she felt his hand stroking her hair, awkwardly and yet gently, she cried all the more. At last she looked up. 'I'm sorry,' she gulped, trying to dry her eyes with her hands. 'I don't know what came over me.'

'You got a fright.' He had taken his hand from her hair, but still squatted on the ground beside her.

'Just because of a butterfly!' She began to laugh a little hysterically. 'Because of a butterfly,' she said

57

again. 'I could have been killed by a snake, and I scare over the sight of a butterfly.' And then she put her hands over her eyes and cried again.

'Delayed shock,' she heard him say. He put his arms around her and held her firmly against him. 'A typical case of delayed shock.'

After a while she stopped crying, but she stayed in the circle of his arms. She could feel the steady beating of his heart, and his closeness was warm and comforting.

'I think you could stand up now,' he said at last.

'Yes, of course,' she said quickly as he dropped his arms, and then, as she raised her tear-stained face to his: 'I must look terrible.'

'How like a female!' He was laughing. 'At least I know you're feeling yourself again. No, Jenny, you don't look in the least awful. You actually look—very pretty.'

He had called her Jenny, she thought wonderingly, as she began to get to her feet. Then she let out a cry of pain, for as she tried to take a step she almost fell once more.

'Jenny! What is it?' He had put out his arm quickly to support her.

'I'm not sure,' she faltered.

'You've hurt yourself?'

'It's my ankle, I think.' Gingerly she tried another step, then winced with pain and leaned on his arm. 'Oh, Ross, I think I've broken my ankle!'

'I hope not.' Ross helped her to lower herself to the ground once more. 'Let me have a look.' He smiled reassuringly up at her. 'I'll try not to hurt

58

you, but don't be brave. If it hurts, you just go ahead and yell.'

'All right,' she murmured, steeling herself to bear the pain as he took hold of her foot and began to investigate. After a moment she really did relax, for he hardly hurt her as he ran his hands expertly but with infinite gentleness over the rapidly swelling foot. All the while Migs, his dog, stood as close to Jenny as she could, nuzzling her with her nose and making small snuffling noises, as if to comfort her.

'A sprain,' Ross pronounced at last. 'A nasty one, but at least the foot isn't broken.'

'Thank goodness for that!' She managed a wan smile.

'Mm.' He straightened and then looked matter-of-factly down at her. 'Now, the next thing to decide—what am I going to do with you?'

'I don't think I can walk,' she ventured.

'That much is obvious. That ankle needs attention.'

'Perhaps you could leave me here and get help. If you went to the hotel they could get a doctor to come to me.'

'And leave you lying here all by yourself?' There was a glimmer of amusement in his eyes.

'The snake!' she exclaimed in horror, remembering.

'I don't imagine it would come this way. We left it sleeping quite peacefully some distance away.'

'In that case . . .' Jenny began.

'I don't like the thought of leaving you here alone,' said Ross. 'In any event, there's no doctor at the hotel. They'd have to send to the nearest town for him. And that takes time.'

'Oh!'

'We're not far from my cottage,' Ross said at last. 'I'll carry you there. Then I'll see what I can do for your ankle.'

'Would you?' she breathed gratefully.

'In case you're worried'—he grinned wickedly—'I *do* know a little about first aid. I'm not a doctor, obviously, but living alone in the backwoods has forced me to pick up some of the basic rudiments of medicine.' He picked up her shoe and placed it unceremoniously in her hands. 'You carry this—it wouldn't fit over the foot right now in any event. And I'll carry you.'

Was it possible to be in heaven in the midst of such pain? Jenny wondered a few minutes later. Then she decided it *was* possible.

'Put your arm round my neck,' Ross had said as he lifted her to him. He held her tightly, the injured foot supported in such a way as to give the least pain. Her face was against his chest, and after a moment or two Jenny let herself relax against him, savouring the feel of the hard-boned chest against her cheek, and the smell that came from his clothes. What was that smell? she wondered. It seemed to be a mixture of resin and pipe smoke and something else which she could not define, all of which blended into a composite male perfume that sent her senses reeling.

'All right?' Ross asked once.

'Perfectly,' she murmured. After that they were silent. Though Jenny was small and slightly built she knew that over a distance she must become heavy, yet Ross walked steadily, without any seeming effort or strain.

All too soon, it seemed to Jenny, they reached the cottage. Ross stopped very near the door. 'Can you open it?' he asked, and when Jenny had leaned forward and pushed the door wide, he carried her through the room she had seen the last time, and into his bedroom. He put her down on his bed, then straightened and took a deep breath. 'All right?' he smiled down at her.

'Fine.' She smiled at him gratefully, and though she knew her face was dirty and tear-stained, she also doubted that she could keep her heart from showing in her eyes. He looked down at her for a long moment, and she saw his eyes deepen in colour. Then he said brusquely, 'Lie back and rest. I'll get together what I need, then we'll see what I can do for that ankle.'

Jenny waited till he had left the room, then she closed her eyes. Though her foot was throbbing she was growing accustomed to the pain. What she had not grown used to was the joy that surged within her. It seemed unbelievable that this strong stern man, with the jagged scar slashing his cheek, could make her feel so lightheaded and happy.

In no time Ross was back. 'I'll try not to hurt you,' he said briefly, as he began to dress her ankle. His movements were calm and unhurried and very expert. 'You're very brave,' he commented once, looking up.

'You're very gentle,' she answered. She could not tell him that the feel of his hands on her skin produced a tingling sensation that even the pain could not still.

At last he said, straightening, 'It may be some time before you're able to run, but at least I've done all I can.'

'Thank you, Mr Sundy,' she said, shy now, for she was uncertain of what would happen next. 'It was really kind of you.'

'Such formality all at once.' His eyes teased her. 'Not at all in keeping after what we've been through.' He paused, and took her hand in his. 'A while back you called me Ross. Let's keep it that way, shall we, Jenny?'

'I'd like that,' she said. 'But, Ross, I still mean the gratitude.'

'Quite unnecessary. I enjoyed carrying you. As for you, Jenny'—his eyes had a wicked gleam— 'was I wrong when I thought that you didn't mind all that much either?'

There was a tenderness in the teasing eyes before which she had to drop her own gaze. She could not even answer his question. Not that it called for a reply, she thought. So she just smiled, conscious that her cheeks were burning.

'As I thought.' Again the teasing note was in his voice. But he made no attempt to prolong the mood, for when he spoke again his tone was matter-of-fact. 'I should think we could both do with something to eat now. How about it, Jenny?'

'Can I cook something?' she asked. 'If you'll tell me where to find things . . .'

'Hold it, lady!' He took a step backwards in

mock alarm. 'An expert job has been done on that ankle, but it's still a fragile thing. You'll have to trust yourself to my cooking. Ever tasted char-grilled fish?' and when she looked at him wonderingly: 'I caught one this morning. You haven't lived till you've eaten char-grilled fish, Jenny.'

Jenny lay back contentedly as a delicious aroma of wood-smoke and cooking fish began to waft through the open window of the room. It did not even occur to her to worry how she would get back to the hotel. Ross would take care of that, just as he would always take care of everything. And then, as she became aware of the significance of her thought, she felt herself grow warm again. Determinedly she pushed the thought from her mind and looked about the room, trying in vain to find some clue to his personality.

Presently Ross was back, carrying a tray.

'We'll eat here?' she asked in surprise.

'I think it would be best in the circumstances.' He was pulling up a chair and table beside the bed. 'One day, I hope, we'll share another meal beneath the trees, but today I want you to stay put and enjoy your food this way.'

Jenny watched Ross putting woven mats on the table, and plates, forks and knives. He was very self-sufficient, she thought. Then he brought the plate of fish and set that down on the table. When he had given her a glass of some exotic-tasting fruit juice, they began to eat.

'Delicious,' she pronounced at last, licking her lips. 'I've never tasted anything so delicious, Ross.'

'I imagine it must be good if I'm to tempt you away from the hotel fare occasionally, Jenny.' Again there was the look which sent the colour flooding into her cheeks. She smiled, and for a time they ate in silence, but it was a companionable silence.

'Have you been doing a lot of walking?' Ross asked after a while.

'Quite a bit, yes.' Jenny told him of a few of the places she had been to.

'There are more,' he observed. 'Perhaps when I have a free day you might like to come out with me? I would take you to places that are off the map, so to speak.'

'Thank you, I'd love that.' She knew her eyes were glowing, and wondered if he realised it was at the thought of spending time with him, rather than the idea of seeing something new.

'Good.' He offered her another piece of fish, and took some himself.

She watched him, thinking only one thing was still necessary to make her happiness complete. 'Ross . . .' she began.

'Jenny?'

'I asked you last time . . . about Neil Donaldson . . .'

'What about Neil Donaldson?' He put his fork abruptly down on his plate, and she saw that the light had left his eyes.

'You . . . you haven't heard anything about him?'

'I told you I hadn't.'

'I just thought I'd ask,' she faltered.

'Jenny,' he said carefully, 'I don't know what

this obsession of yours is all about. All I can tell you is there's no forester called Neil Donaldson anywhere around here.'

'I'm sorry.' She looked at him miserably, upset that she had destroyed the lovely atmosphere that had existed between them.

'Nothing to be sorry about,' he said abruptly.

'You seem so annoyed . . .' she faltered.

'I'm not annoyed. It's just that I told you once before there was nobody here by that name. I don't feel like discussing the matter again.' He took up her glass, refilled it and passed it to her. 'Good for growing girls,' he said lightly, but she saw that though he was smiling there was still a hint of strain in his eyes.

They went on eating, and while they ate they talked, and after a time Jenny observed with relief that the strain had vanished. Presently Ross glanced at his watch. 'It's so pleasant having you here, Jenny, that I would like to keep you with me for much longer. But I imagine your friend at the hotel will begin to worry about you.'

'Mrs Ramsden!' Jenny clapped her hand to her mouth and looked contrite. 'Do you know, I'd been enjoying this meal so much I'd forgotten all about her.'

'Even with a sprained ankle?' teased Ross, and Jenny was glad to see the twinkle reappear in his eyes.

'It was the fish I enjoyed,' she said with pretended demureness. 'Ross, I'll have to start getting back.' She tried to get to her feet, but as the bandaged foot touched the ground she winced with pain.

'And how do you propose getting back?' Ross asked with amusement.

'I . . . perhaps you could cut me two branches from one of these trees. We could trim them a little, make them into crutches. I could probably manage that way,' she said bravely.

'I can just see you hopping all the way back to the hotel!' Ross chuckled, and then, seeing the hurt expression in her eyes, he stretched across the table and took her hand in his. 'Jenny, Jenny, my sweet, can you see me letting you do it?'

'Then . . .' She was a little breathless. There had been a look of tenderness in his eyes when he had used the endearment that caught at her heart. 'Oh, Ross, I'm so silly. Of course—you must have a car. And there must be a motor road down the mountain.'

'There *is* a road,' he said, 'but unfortunately my car is in town for a service.'

'What shall I do, then?' she asked.

'You'll go back the same way as you came here,' he said slowly. 'I'll have to carry you.'

'You can't mean that!' she said incredulously.

'I don't see what else we can do.'

'But, Ross, it's so far. When I fell we were near your cottage. But from here to the hotel—why, it's more than an hour's walk.'

'Hm, you have a point.' He was silent a moment. 'Jenny, I have it!'

'You have?'

'The perfect answer. Stay right here. I'll be with you in a minute.'

He was back in the room a few minutes later. His face was alight with mischief so that he looked more like a naughty boy than a grown man. 'Ma'am, your Rolls is waiting,' he announced, and he lifted her ceremoniously from the bed and carried her outside. Beside the cottage door stood a wheelbarrow, battered and ancient.

'Oh, Ross!' Jenny laughed so much that she choked.

'Ma'am is displeased?' he asked in pretended dismay. 'The honourable vehicle may look a little old, but I can assure Ma'am it's roadworthy.'

'It's priceless, Ross. You'll really wheel me back in it?'

'Certainly. I'm a man of many parts—mender of ankles, cook, wheelbarrow-pusher. Ma'am is ready?' He dumped her in the wheelbarrow.

They started on their way. It was a merry journey through the forest. The path was clear and well kept, and Ross had little trouble pushing the wheelbarrow down the mountain. In the jungle things became a little more difficult. Here the path was so overgrown that it took much longer to negotiate the wheelbarrow over the gnarled roots and stones.

Once the wheels caught in a knotted mass of roots and jerked so violently that Ross, caught off his guard, let go of the handles, and Jenny spilled out of the barrow. She was nearly on the ground when he caught her. They were laughing so much that for a moment neither of them could breathe. 'Jenny! Jenny, you're all right?' Ross gasped at last.

'Yes,' she gasped. 'I didn't have far to fall.'

'Then Ma'am will not dismiss her humble servant?' He was holding her, and then, when she had regained her balance and thought he would help her back into the barrow, she felt his arms tighten around her. 'Jenny,' he said very softly, and now there was no trace of laughter in his voice. 'Oh, Jenny!' She felt his lips touch her hair. Then he helped her back into the barrow and they went further.

When they came out of the jungle into the sun, Ross stopped to wipe his brow. It had been a difficult stretch, long and laborious, and Jenny's heart went out to him when she saw how tired he looked.

The track was easier now, and Ross was able to push with more ease. Sometimes when the road sloped downwards and the surface was smooth, he would leave go of the handles for a moment or two, and laugh to see Jenny's look of consternation as she wondered if she would fall out. There was a streak of mischief in him that Neil would have liked, she thought. But she knew better than to mention Neil's name again.

They came to the stream and Jenny wondered how Ross proposed getting over it. 'Easy,' he announced. He plucked her out of the barrow, told her to put her arms around his neck, then carried her quickly and easily from boulder to boulder. Reaching the path on the other side, he set her down on the sand, went back across the stream for the wheelbarrow, and then they were on their way once more.

'Whatever will Mrs Ramsden think when she sees me arriving like this?' said Jenny, when she saw the hotel buildings in the distance.

'She'll think her companion turned into a load of dry leaves.' The remark was so ridiculous that it started them laughing again. They were still laughing when they reached the hotel.

An amused audience gathered about them and accompanied them on their way up the drive. Mrs Ramsden appeared suddenly from the garden, concerned and anxious, but one look at Jenny's merry eyes reassured her.

Momentarily, on the edge of the crowd, Jenny caught sight of Ann, the hotel receptionist. The girl's face was cold and unfriendly. Jenny glanced at Ross, but he did not appear to have seen her.

At the door of the bungalow Ross helped Jenny out of the wheelbarrow. With Mrs Ramsden supporting her on one side and Ross on the other, Jenny was able to hop inside. When she was settled on her bed Ross did not linger. He looked at his watch, smiled, and said goodbye.

# CHAPTER FIVE

The day after Jenny's mishap Andrew was driving
his mother into town to make some purchases, and
Mrs Ramsden insisted that Jenny go with them to
see a doctor. Though Jenny thought it unnecessary
Mrs Ramsden was so concerned that she had to
give in.

When the doctor had taken the dressing from
her foot and examined it thoroughly he confirmed
what Ross had said. It was badly sprained, but
there was no fracture. As he re-dressed the ankle
he commented on the expertise with which it had
been treated. 'It was obviously done by someone
with a good knowledge of first aid,' he said. 'And
as a result you'll be up and about again much
sooner than you would otherwise have been.' He
warned Jenny to take things easy and not try to
walk too soon. 'Since you tell me you'll be here
for quite some time you'll have lots more opportunity
to go exploring.'

When Andrew heard what the doctor had said,
he stopped at a bookshop and bought Jenny some
reading matter, and his mother gave her a present

of a traycloth and gay embroidery cottons to work it with.

'Isn't embroidery for elderly ladies?' Andrew laughed when he saw it.

'Not at all,' said Mrs Langley, giving him a look which Jenny did not miss. 'Most young girls like to get things ready for their bottom drawer.'

'Hm.' Andrew looked at Jenny thoughtfully for a moment, and then, to her relief, changed the subject.

Though Jenny was forced to take things easy, the time passed pleasantly enough. The hotel guests all liked the pretty young girl with the violet eyes and the fair hair, and at one time or another most of them found time to sit with her in the garden and chat.

The garden was very beautiful, with its profusion of exotic shrubs and flowers, and the lovely view into the mountains, and Jenny knew she could spend her enforced leisure time quite happily. She enjoyed doing the embroidery Mrs Langley had given her, for she was always happy when her hands were busy. She spent happy hours doing sketches of the mountains which never ceased to fascinate her. Where at first the escarpment had seemed one entity, now she had begun to recognise the different mountains that surrounded the hotel. She began to see how each peak had its own particular formation and colouring, how each had a definite character of its own.

Much of Jenny's time was spent reading. The books Andrew had given her were interesting ones, yet often she would find herself looking up from the pages, her eyes on the mountains, her thoughts far away.

Had she fallen in love with Ross? Jenny wondered about this more and more since the eventful day she had spent with him. She tried to tell herself that what she felt was no more than a passing infatuation, that it could not have grown into an emotion so deep that she was not certain how to cope with it.

In any event, the relationship could hold no promise of permanence. In less than three months Mrs Ramsden would be returning to England, and Jenny would have to go with her. England was where her life was. A passing infatuation could not be enough to keep her from going back home.

Thoughts of Ross often led her to wonder about Ann. As much as the attitude of the other guests had become friendly and protective, so Ann's hostility had grown. Jenny envied the other girl her position, for when she herself went back to England Ann would still be here. Ann was obviously fond of Ross. Did she love him? And how did he feel about her? Had he looked at her also with tenderness in his eyes? There were men who did this, she knew, men who could make every girl they spoke to feel special. She did not think Ross was the type—yet she did not know him well enough to be certain.

One morning, when Jenny was alone in the garden, she decided to write to Lynn. Despite the fact that she had been writing to her regularly, Jenny's letters were usually about Lynn's mother and how much they both were enjoying the mountains. She had never mentioned the mystery concerning Neil.

The more her feelings for Ross had grown, the more she had tried to convince herself that any mystery was of her own making. But in her rational moments she knew she could not dismiss the wariness which came into Ross's face at mention of the other man. She could not dismiss the near certainty that he knew more than he was prepared to say.

What could it be? The thought came to her one day that it was possible that Neil had in fact been a forester; that he might have disgraced himself in some way and been forced to leave. But Neil would never do anything wrong on purpose. It was so long since she had seen him, but she was certain the boy she had known could not have grown into a man who was dishonest or destructive.

Perhaps he was in trouble. All those years ago, when Jenny had been a child, Neil had been the one to help her. Was he now the one in need?

Jenny considered carefully what she should say to Lynn. Perhaps Mrs Ramsden had already mentioned Jenny's suspicions in letters to her daughter. She did not want to sound obsessed or neurotic. After all, the Drakensberg was an extremely long range of mountains, hundreds of miles in extent. It was not impossible that Lynn had in fact got the story wrong, that Neil was a forester in another district; that the Stewarts, who had seen him, had met him somewhere altogether different.

Taking up her pen at last, she told Lynn, as casually as she was able to word it, that Neil did not appear to be known in the district, and that she wondered whether the Stewarts could have met him somewhere else. When she gave the letter to Mrs Ramsden for posting, she did not mention what was in it. Lynn's reply would take some time to arrive, and until then, Jenny told herself sensibly, she would try to think no more about the matter.

In the evenings Andrew kept her entertained. It was comfortable to be with a person who did not set her pulses racing each time he was near, Jenny thought. And Andrew was such good fun—always friendly, never moody, never too tired to sit with her by the fire and talk. He told her of his training, and of how he managed to go further and do more difficult climbs all the time. He told her of expeditions he had been on, of countries and animals and people and customs she had never dreamed existed. He had the gift of making his descriptions live, so that Jenny was never bored.

Often she would find the eyes of Mrs Ramsden and Mrs Langley on them, but this had ceased to worry her. She was doing nothing wrong. She made no pretence of leading Andrew on—indeed Andrew himself gave no indication of being interested in anything but a friendly and completely platonic relationship.

Not every evening was spent talking. Sometimes there was a film, and even if it was one that Jenny had seen long ago, before her parents became ill, it was a diversion. Andrew found an old Monopoly, and the four of them spent merry evenings negotiating lively property deals over the battered old board.

So the evening hours sped by pleasantly. Only at night, when Jenny was in bed and the room in darkness, did the feelings of restlessness assail her. Perhaps her emotions were heightened by the vista of stars outside her window, or by the lovely perfumes that drifted in from the garden. Whatever the cause, she only knew that the feeling of longing, of wanting to see Ross again, grew so unbearable that often at sunrise her pillow was wet.

One morning Jenny and Mrs. Ramsden were sitting in the garden. They had just finished their tea, Mrs Ramsden had taken up her knitting, and Jenny was trying to capture a scene that seemed to be eluding her.

A shadow fell across the page and she looked up. For a moment she could not speak. He had caught her so completely off guard that she had no time to hide the emotions which surged up in her at sight of the stern-faced figure in the neat safari suit.

' Ross!' she exclaimed. ' Oh, Ross, it's you!'

' Hello, Jenny.' His face had not relaxed. Only his eyes seemed to soften at the sight of her obvious emotion.

' Ross,' she said again, and just looked at him helplessly.

He smiled suddenly and said, ' Well, Jenny, should I go, or may I sit down and join you?'

' My manners!' she gasped, and without thinking she tried to jump up.

' Steady!' He pushed her gently back into the chair. ' That foot must be fragile still,' he laughed softly, 'and I don't have my wheelbarrow with me today.'

'Oh, Ross!' Now she too was laughing, her confusion vanished with his jest. 'I'm an idiot. Please sit down.' She turned to Mrs Ramsden who had been watching the interchange with great interest. 'Mrs Ramsden, this is Mr Sundy.'

'We've met,' said Mrs Ramsden. 'Don't you remember the day Mr Sundy helped you down the mountain?'

'I hope you don't mind me joining you, Mrs Ramsden?' Ross spoke courteously, inclining his head towards the older woman.

'It's nice for Jenny to have company.' Mrs Ramsden's voice was friendly, but to Jenny's ears it lacked some of its usual warmth. 'Jenny dear, if we catch a waiter's eye we could order a fresh pot of tea. Mr Sundy must be feeling tired and hot.'

'Thank you.' He smiled at her. 'But I've just had a beer.'

'Well, in that case . . .' She glanced at her watch. 'I've just remembered, Jenny—I must go and finish a letter. The post leaves in half an hour.' She bent to pick up her bag, put in her glasses and her knitting, and then got to her feet. 'You'll excuse me, won't you, Mr Sundy?'

'She thinks she must be tactful,' Jenny said, watching her go.

'Sensible woman.' Ross pushed his chair closer to hers. 'I wanted to be alone with you. How are you, Jenny?'

He really wanted to know, she thought wonderingly. It was not just a courtesy question. 'I'm getting on well,' she said.

'I'm glad. I've thought of you often, but it's the first chance I've had to get here. We had a spot of bother in the forest and I couldn't get away.'

'Oh!' So it was not that he had not wanted to come.

'Are you able to walk yet, Jenny?'

Jenny felt at that moment that if happiness alone could propel her along the ground, she could probably out-distance the fleetest deer. 'A little,' she said. 'Though till now I've had to use these crutches to get from the room to the garden.'

'Did you see a doctor?'

'Yes—the day after the accident someone took me into town and the doctor there had a look at my foot.'

'And was it a sprain?'

'Yes.' She smiled. 'The doctor complimented you on the way you'd looked after me, Ross.'

'I'm glad to hear it,' he said with a grin. 'But I'm even happier to hear that you're better. I've a proposition to put to you, Jenny. But first, I want to see you walk.'

'A proposition?' She glanced at him curiously.

'Not the kind that would give your friend Mrs Ramsden the shudders, although'—his eyes were teasing—'that kind of proposition would give me no end of pleasure too.'

'What kind of proposition?' she asked, ignoring the implication of his words.

'Let me see you walk.'

'Oh, Ross!' She pretended to pout. 'You are a tyrant. Did anybody ever tell you that?' She got to her feet, taking her weight off the injured foot with acquired practice. Slowly she hobbled from her chair to a tree a few yards away.

'Far enough,' she heard him calling. 'Don't walk right out of my life.'

'Would you mind?' she asked, before she could stop herself, and felt her cheeks grow warm under his level gaze.

'Yes, Jenny,' he said after a long moment. 'You know I would.'

'Oh, well . . .' She was a little breathless as she hobbled back to him—a breathlessness which owed little to physical exertion. 'You've seen me walk. You said something about a proposition?'

'I have a free day tomorrow. Would you like to spend it with me?' And as she gazed at him, her eyes glowing : 'I thought we might go for a picnic.'

'I'd like that,' she said. 'Where would we go?'

'A surprise,' he said enigmatically.

'It's just—I can't walk very far. You might not enjoy it . . .'

'I have my car back, so we won't have to rely on a wheelbarrow. There won't be much walking, Jenny, and you've satisfied me that you *can* do a few steps on your own. But if you really can't manage'—his expression set her heart pounding once more—'I've a pair of fairly strong arms, you know.'

'Yes,' she said after a moment, very softly, 'I do know.'

'Then you'll come?'

'Of course I will.'

'Good.' There was a look a real satisfaction in his face.

'What shall I bring?' she asked.

'Let me see,' he said, pretending to think. 'I have enough food and drink, so I think—yes, I think your contribution need be—just yourself.'

'Oh, Ross!' She could not help laughing. 'You're so good for me.'

'I'm glad, Jenny.' Glancing at his watch, he got to his feet. 'Have to be getting along now. Till tomorrow, then. About nine?'

'I'll be ready,' she promised.

She watched him walk away, the tall lithe figure in the safari suit, his legs athletic and muscled, his arms deep brown from the sun. Was it only a few days ago that she had thought she could prevent herself from falling in love with him?

She was still smiling when Mrs Ramsden rejoined her in the garden. 'I saw Mr Sundy leaving,' she said quietly.

'Yes.' Jenny turned warmly to the older woman. 'Thank you for pretending you had letters to write. I realised it was an excuse, but I appreciated it.'

'You appreciated it,' Mrs Ramsden said slowly, with an unexpected look of concern. 'I suppose you did. And yet, Jenny, I can't help wondering whether I did the right thing.'

'You needn't have done it,' Jenny said quickly. 'Nothing we spoke about was secret. But it was a lovely thing to do all the same.' She hardly noticed the other woman's silence, her mind busy with the next day's delights. 'Mrs Ramsden, Ross asked me to go for a picnic with him tomorrow.'

'Jenny . . .' the look of concern had deepened, 'I wonder if that's wise?'

'You mean because of my foot?'

'I . . .'

'It's much better, you know. I can walk small distances without crutches now.'

'Yes . . .' said Mrs Ramsden slowly.

'In fact, Ross made me show him how I walked before he put the proposition to me.'

'Proposition?'

'Ross's word.' Jenny laughed. 'I don't know why I used it just now. I must be very impressionable.'

'Yes. Yes, I think you may be. Jenny, my dear,' said Mrs Ramsden carefully, 'I wonder if it's a good idea to go with Mr Sundy?'

'But . . .' Jenny looked bewildered. 'Of course I won't go if there's something you would rather I did with you tomorrow . . .'

'No, my dear, it's not that.'

'I know you're worried about my foot. You're a darling, Mrs Ramsden, but you needn't worry. I'm much better now, really I am. Anyway, Ross said we'd be going by car. He thought I'd manage the bit of walking there might be. He said even if I couldn't manage . . .' She stopped abruptly, her cheeks betraying her treacherously once more.

'Jenny,' Mrs Ramsden began, as if she were about to say something, then stopped as she thought better of it. Finally she said gently, 'It's all there in your face, my dear. Anyone who knows you well could see it.'

'I . . .' Jenny opened her mouth to speak, but there was nothing to say. She lifted her hand in a hopeless gesture and dropped it into her lap once more.

'I was so hoping you would get to like Andrew,' Mrs Ramsden said, after a long silence.

'But I do,' Jenny said quickly. 'I'm so fond of Andrew. Really I am.'

'Fond? Yes, Jenny, I know you're fond of him. But,' she looked at her sadly, 'you don't love him, do you?'

'I haven't known him very long,' the girl said a little desperately, wondering that a glorious morning could turn sour so swiftly.

'No. And yet you haven't known Mr Sundy long either.'

'No.'

'Do you love him, Jenny?' Mrs Ramsden's eyes were distressed. 'There—I've said it! You'll think me an interfering old woman, and no doubt I am . . .'

'Oh, no,' Jenny protested. 'You could never be that.'

'I have your interests at heart, my dear. I'm so fond of you. You know how much I want to see you happy.'

'But I *am* happy. Happier than I've been for so long.'

'I know.' Impulsively Mrs Ramsden stretched out a hand to the girl. 'I told you—it's all there in your face for me to read. You're quite radiant.' She paused, then said gently, 'Jenny dear, I wish you'd consider. This man—Mr Sundy—what is he?'

'A forester.' Jenny looked pleadingly at the other woman.

'A forester?' Mrs Ramsden echoed.

'You say that as if he's nothing!'

'Oh, no!'

'But he is,' Jenny insisted. 'He had to study to become a forester. You've only to hear him speak to know that he's clever. He . . . he's a fine man, Mrs Ramsden.'

'Perhaps. But, Jenny, your life is in England. It's where you belong.'

'Andrew doesn't live in England, and you would be glad if I were to marry him.'

'That's true.' Mrs Ramsden looked unhappy. 'I'm not being very consistent. But Andrew . . . Andrew is different, Jenny. He . . . he's so eligible.'

'It's not enough. I couldn't marry a man just because he was eligible.'

'Perhaps not.' Mrs Ramsden sighed. 'You still haven't answered my question. I've no right to ask it, Jenny, but . . .'

'Which question?' Jenny asked tonelessly.

'About Mr Sundy.'

It was almost midday. A heat haze shimmered and danced over a clump of rocks. Bees droned in the flowers and a vivid yellow bird sang cheekily in a nearby tree. Jenny's eyes were on the mountains, as if she would find the answer she sought on the rugged tree-covered slopes.

At last she turned her head slowly and looked at Mrs Ramsden. 'Yes, I love him,' she said very softly. 'I love Ross.' She was silent again, her fingers playing nervously with her sketch-pencil. When she spoke once more her tone was deliberately bright. 'I love him, but that doesn't mean he loves me, or that he would ever marry me. Ross is very self-sufficient. Perhaps he'll never get married at all.'

'Then you will go tomorrow?'

'It's just a picnic.' If only Mrs Ramsden had not made such an issue of the invitation! 'The fact that I'm going to spend the day with Ross doesn't mean a thing.'

'Perhaps you're right.' Mrs Ramsden picked up her knitting. 'Jenny, what about Neil?'

'What about him?' Jenny's eyes were troubled, for she sensed what the older woman would say.

'You thought Mr Sundy was keeping something back.'

'That's true.'

'And now you think differently?'

Why are you doing this to me? Jenny wanted to say, and knew she could not, for Mrs Ramsden was trying, in the only way she knew, to help her. 'I can't answer that question,' she said, 'but I don't believe Ross would ever do anything bad or dishonest.'

'Do you still think there's some mystery about Neil's whereabouts?'

Jenny stared bleakly into the mountains. At last she said honestly, 'Yes. Yes, I do. But I don't think'—she turned quickly to Mrs Ramsden—'and you must believe me—I don't think Ross is mixed up in it.'

'I hope you're right.' Mrs Ramsden came to the

end of her row, and took out a tape measure to see how much she had done. Jenny had the feeling that she was giving herself time to think. When she looked up at last her eyes were as warm and smiling as always. 'Go out with him tomorrow, Jenny,' she said. 'And have a good time. You deserve it.'

# CHAPTER SIX

Long before the sun was up next morning Jenny was awake. She was so eager to see whether or not it would be a fine day that she jumped out of bed, forgetting her foot, and then, as her weight sank down on it, she grimaced with sudden pain. But after a moment she was able to hobble to the window.

It was dark still and the air was cold. The sky was an opaque grey, and the mountain peaks a darker grey silhouetted against it. Where, Jenny wondered, would Ross take her? He had said it would be a surprise. And then, looking at the mountains, so mysterious in the lifting darkness, she knew it did not matter where they went. All that mattered was that she would be with him. A whole day stretched out before her, a day spent alone with Ross. The very thought was bliss.

The eastern sky grew lighter. Jenny had opened the window so that she could enjoy the lovely perfumes that drifted in from the garden, but now she became conscious of the cold air that filtered in from outside, creeping beneath her nightie, and turning her bare feet to ice.

It was still some hours before breakfast, but though the thought of her warm bed was tempting, Jenny could not get back beneath the blankets. She was too excited, too restless. Very quietly, so as not to waken Mrs Ramsden, she went to the cupboard and thought about what she would wear. Then she hobbled silently from the room to have her bath.

She was in the garden when Ross came for her. She had eaten her breakfast rapidly, hardly tasting her food. Now she sat with a book on her lap in the garden, wondering when he would come.

A hundred times she looked up, expecting to see him, chiding herself mentally for being worse than a child awaiting a treat. She must be sensible about this outing, she told herself, lifting her book and starting to read. After all, it was nothing more than a picnic. But hardly had she read a few lines, her eyes skimming the words and her mind not taking in their meaning, when she would hear the snapping of a twig or the rustle of grass, and would turn her head quickly to see if it was Ross.

Finally he came. Jenny's heart lifted when she saw the tall figure striding towards her. He was not dressed in his usual safari suit, but was wearing shorts and a navy sports shirt, open at the neck. He looked so vital that she wondered how she could have thought him middle-aged even for a moment.

'Jenny,' he said, smiling down at her. 'Have you been waiting long?'

'Not long at all.' Now that he was here it was as if the waiting had never been.

'Let me help you up.' He stooped to take her

arm.

'I'm all right, really I am,' she laughed protestingly.

'Have to watch you.' His touch was gentle, but it sent the inevitable ripples of excitement along her arm. 'I want you to enjoy the day—you won't if your foot plays up.'

When she was standing he held her away from him. 'Let me look at you,' he said. After much deliberation she had decided to wear cream-coloured slacks with a pink blouse that enhanced her fair colouring. She knew that she looked her best. 'Very nice,' said Ross after a long moment.

Jenny would be seeing a different part of the mountains today, he told her as he began to drive. It was a lovely day. The sky was a deep blue with wisps of white cloud hovering over the tips of the peaks. There had been some rain recently, and the countryside was green, almost lush in parts. The road climbed and twisted, and at every turn of the way new vistas lay before them. Once, when they came to a place where the road had been widened to allow people to admire the view, Ross stopped the car. The view was so breathtaking that Jenny gazed about her, quite unable to speak. The morning mist had lifted, and the mountains folded upon one another in a never-ending line of peaks and overlapping slopes. Far below, in a gorge that wound between the mountains, Jenny saw the glint of a river, and at the side of the road a profusion of wild flowers, orange and white and yellow, danced and swayed in the breeze. Over everything hung an aura of serenity and of vastness.

'Like it?' Ross had moved closer to her, his arm stretched out along the top of the seat behind her.

She turned to him, nodding wordlessly. Her eyes were moist, her emotion heightened because he was there to share the beauty with her. 'I thought you would.' His voice was gruff and the arm that rested on the seat closed about her. Jenny did not know how long they sat there, in a nearness that needed no words. She only knew that when he took his arm from her shoulders so that he could start the car once more, she was filled with a strange sense of loss.

They had their picnic beside a river-pool. It was a quiet and lovely place to which Ross brought her, a place that was so far off the beaten track that visitors to the mountains seldom discovered it, he told her. The sun filtering through the tall trees threw dappled shadows on the rocks. Over a sheer cliff face hurtled a waterfall, a rushing mass of white foam which fell into the pool where Jenny and Ross were sitting. Moss clung to the rocks, and beneath the trees Jenny saw hundreds of toadstools. 'Poisonous,' Ross cautioned her when he saw her eyes on them. 'Not to be eaten.'

'I know. But aren't they pretty!' Jenny turned to him, laughing. 'Look at those red ones, with the white spots. They came here straight out of a fairy story. Do you know, Ross, I think you've brought me to a fairy glen. If I close my eyes the fairies will come out from behind those toadstools and begin to dance.'

'You're still a little girl in many ways, aren't you?'

Ross reached out and rumpled her hair. He was laughing, but in his eyes was a look she could not define. 'Did you believe in fairies when you were a child, Jenny?'

'Of course. Doesn't every child?' Unbidden a picture of Neil came into her mind, laughing away her fears of goblins when they had been in a dark part of the woods. But that was long ago. Determinedly she thrust the picture from her mind. She would not think of Neil today, for if she did she might end up talking about him, and then she knew Ross's face would cloud, and the lovely day would be spoiled.

'Hungry?' Ross was grinning at her. He looked so carefree and content that she was glad she had not mentioned Neil.

'Starving!'

'As I thought.' He had brought a haversack with him, and Jenny watched curiously as he opened it, wondering what was in it. 'First,' he said, 'I'm going to cool our drink.' He took bottles of orange juice and immersed them in the icy mountain water. 'That will take care of your thirst when you get hot,' he informed her. Then he took a packet of sandwiches and put them out on a cardboard plate. 'We'll have these now. Just an appetiser, I'll leave the rest in the bag for later.'

'Delicious,' she said, when she had taken a bite of her sandwich. 'You're very self-sufficient, aren't you, Ross?'

'I've had to be,' he said quietly.

'Have you never wanted to marry?' The moment

she had asked the question she could have bitten her tongue. But perhaps he had not taken her words as a hint.

'I'm not a confirmed bachelor, if that's what you mean,' Ross said slowly. 'But what girl would share the life of a forester? It can be very lonely.'

He was watching her so intently that she had to drop her eyes. 'There must be girls who would like it,' she said hesitantly, trying to sound casual.

'Ah, but any girl wouldn't do,' he said. 'I don't need a housekeeper. When I marry it will be only if the girl I love wants to share this life . . .' His voice trailed away and his eyes held a distant look. Jenny sensed that he was thinking of a particular girl, and felt a stab of pain wrench inside her.

Abruptly he changed the subject. 'Do you know how to make a stone skim the water?' he asked, bending to choose a pebble. He stood up, went to the edge of the water, and with an effortless movement he let the pebble go. Jenny watched it skim gently and swiftly over the surface of the pool, the water just rippling slightly with its movement.

'Easy,' she said, glad of the diversion. Picking up a stone, she imitated his movement. The stone plopped into the water and sank.

'Oh, dear,' Jenny sighed, after yet another of her stones had sunk to the bottom. 'I can't do it. You'd think the fairies in this glen could lend a hand.'

'You don't need fairies. I'll show you.' He came close to her, took her arm and made a throwing movement. 'Like this. Think you can do it?'

'I'll try.' A little breathlessly, she bent, chose a pebble, and this time the movement must have been better, for though the pebble did not skim as Ross's did, it did not sink with the obstinacy of her previous efforts.

'Excellent! Again, Jenny.' He was delighted. 'I'll make a pebble-skimmer of you yet.'

As she bent to choose another stone she looked up at him. His eyes were twinkling with mischief. His face, so often stern and serious, was relaxed and boyish. This was how she loved him most—when the playful mood was upon him. To prolong it she fell in with his mood, and sent yet another pebble skipping over the water.

After a while they grew tired of this game. They began to talk, and Jenny marvelled at how much they found to discuss, and at how much they had in common.

Presently Ross began to talk about the mountains and the forests. He told her of his duties as a forester. He told her of the trees that grew on the slopes of the mountains, of the bushes and the wild flowers and the birds. His eyes were bright, his face rapt. And as Jenny watched his face and listened to his words she began to understand how much his work meant to him. This was his life, and he loved it.

She did not know how long they had been talking when he looked up at the sun and said, ' That tummy of yours must be getting hungry again.'

'I'm always hungry here. Ross, you looked at the sun—can you tell the time that way?'

'Sometimes I forget I have a watch on me.' He

leaped over the rocks and leaned into the pool where he had put the bottle of juice. He came back to where she was sitting, and held the bottle against her cheek, suddenly, without warning.

The cold hit her with a shock and she gave a yell. 'Beast!'

'Just demonstrating the effectiveness of our mountain refrigeration.' He grinned at her as he began to unpack the haversack.

'That was gorgeous!' she sighed a little while later, when they had finished their lunch of chicken sandwiches, fruit and orange juice.

'I'm glad.' Ross was putting the debris into a packet which then went back into the haversack. 'Did you enjoy it enough to come again?'

Her glowing eyes were the only answer he needed. He looked at her for a long moment, his eyes gleaming with satisfaction. Then he stretched out a hand to her. 'Come, Jenny, I think it's time we went.'

Walking down to the river had not been too difficult for her. At one point she had sat on a rock and simply slithered down. But she found that getting back up was an entirely different proposition. She watched Ross jump from rock to rock, nimble-footed and sure of himself, and knew that even at the best of times, when she had no injuries to hinder her, she could not match him. He turned all at once, saw her difficulty, and grinned. He took the haversack from his shoulders, put it on the ground, then went back to her. 'Sorry, Jenny, I forgot you needed help. You managed so well coming down.'

'I slid down,' she said ruefully.

'And the law of gravity defies you to slide back up again.' His eyes shone with mischief. 'Hold on tightly now.' And with a quick movement, as if she were no heavier than a parcel of feathers, he had lifted her in his arms and was climbing over the rocks with her.

Her heart was beating wildly as she felt the hardness of his body against her own. It was like that other time, she thought, only then she had not wanted to admit to herself that she loved him. This time she simply gave herself up to the feelings of the moment.

At the top of the rocks he stopped. 'I can walk now,' she said, a little breathlessly.

'I know.' His voice was gruff. He was still holding her, and the mischief had vanished from his eyes as he stood there, quite still, staring down into her face. For a long heart-stopping moment they looked at each other. Then he lifted her closer towards him and she felt his lips touch her hair. 'Jenny,' he whispered once, very softly. Then he put her down.

The car was not far away, and they walked the rest of the way in silence. 'It's been a lovely day,' she said later, when they reached the hotel.

'The first of many, I hope,' said Ross. 'Goodbye, Jenny.' He had opened the door for her, and as he helped her out of the car he drew her close. Again she felt the feather-light touch of his lips on her hair.

She did not know how long she stood there, watching him drive away. Only when she heard a voice behind

93

her did she turn. 'Miss Windham'—it was Ann, the receptionist—'I'm glad to see you're feeling better.'

'Thank you.' Jenny looked at the other girl, wondering at the hard bright look in the pretty eyes. Had Ann seen her with Ross? If so, this might be the reason for her hostility. At Ann's next words her suspicions were confirmed.

'It must be nice for you to get around once more,' she was saying. 'And with Ross to drive you, you don't need to walk much, do you?'

'Not all that much,' Jenny agreed, a little coolly, stung by the other girl's manner.

'What more can you ask for?' Ann said blandly, her voice smooth as silk. 'The sympathy of all the guests *and* a scenic tour with an expert who knows all the best places. He *does* know the best places, doesn't he?'

'Does he?' Jenny said as casually as she could. 'I can't tell you from my personal experience. I haven't been to many yet.'

'Ah, but you will. Ross always knows the places girls will like.'

'He . . .' Jenny bit off her words, annoyed with herself that she had risen to Ann's bait and been about to ask more.

'You were going to ask?'

'Nothing,' Jenny said flatly.

'Sure?' She waited a moment, but when Jenny did not answer she said, 'You'll be taking part tonight, of course?'

'Taking part?' Jenny looked bewildered. What

on earth was Ann getting at now?

'The fancy dress. After supper—in the lounge.' Ann smiled again, her eyes like diamonds in the pretty face. 'You must have seen the notice board.'

'There was something . . .' Jenny began guiltily. The excitement of seeing Ross again had crowded out all other thoughts. Only now that Ann mentioned it did she remember seeing the notice.

'We're having a book fancy dress party. Everyone will come dressed as a fiction character or a book-title. We did so hope that all our guests would be taking part.' Ann gave a brittle laugh. 'In any event, Mr Langley probably saw the notice and would have reminded you, so even if you had forgotten you wouldn't have missed it.'

'I suppose not.' Now Jenny turned deliberately and began to walk slowly in the direction of the bungalow.

The receptionist really had her own brand of nastiness. It should not bother her—and yet it did. It was obvious that Ann was attracted to Ross. Indeed, it was hard to imagine any girl remaining unaffected by him. But did Ann need to be so nasty? The insinuation that Ross was attentive to many girls—did that mean anything? She wanted so much to believe the remark stemmed only as a result of Ann's hostility. But the remark was insidious. Now that it had been made she must try not to brood about it. As for the remark about Andrew—what had that been all about?

Jenny was tired. It had been a long day, a lovely day, but she had walked more than she had done since hurting her foot, and now it was throbbing. More than anything she wanted to go to her room and rest. If she could have done so she would willingly have forgone her supper and crept straight into bed. But she knew that Mrs Ramsden, though she would say nothing to object, would be hurt. There was nothing for it—after a rest and a shower she would have to start getting ready for supper.

Mrs Ramsden was not in the bungalow, and Jenny was glad. She lay back on her bed and tried to think. She loved reading, and normally she would have enjoyed the evening that lay ahead. There were so many fictional characters that she could think of, but each required a certain amount of preparation—and she had no time.

Clearly she would have to think quickly. At last she remembered a book she had once read, *The Egg and I*. She took her writing pad, detached the cardboard page at the end of it and drew on it the shape of an egg. Then she took her scissors, cut around the outlined shape and with her sketching crayons she coloured it in. Then she pinned the egg to her cardigan with a safety-pin.

After dinner Jenny and Mrs Ramsden went into the lounge. Already the room was a buzz of anticipation, and as Jenny looked at the people all around her, she felt a pang of remorse. Most of them had been to so much trouble. Their costumes had been created with care and ingenuity. Though the judging had not yet begun, many of the guests were walking about, guessing titles and characters, and complimenting one another on their originality.

Although she really did not feel up to it, Jenny tried to fit in with the mood of the evening. Mrs Ramsden's look of disappointment when she had seen the girl's attempt at a fancy dress had not been lost on her. 'That's sweet,' she had commented after a quick glance at the little piece of cardboard on Jenny's cardigan. Then she had changed the subject. Mrs Ramsden herself had gone to a great deal of trouble, and she must have felt that the girl could have done likewise.

They were sitting near the fire when they were joined by Andrew and his mother. Mrs Langley was dressed as the Queen from *Alice in Wonderland*, and Andrew looked very dashing as Robin Hood. From somewhere he had managed to dig up a tyrolean hat, green with a sprightly feather, and he wore a green jerkin over tight-fitting trousers. There was even a bow, well equipped with arrows, which he had made from supple twigs.

Presently the judging began. As each person passed before the judges the other guests would try to guess what they represented. When the title or character had been confirmed there would be a round of applause, and it was by the volume of applause that the winners were determined. Many of the representations were easy to guess, but some were not. When this happened the person gave an explanation for the costume, and when the audience saw how apt it was, the clapping was often very great.

When Andrew went up to be judged the lounge rang with noise. Added to the fact that he was popular, he made such a handsome and dashing figure in his Robin Hood get-up.

Then it was Jenny's turn. The title of her book was guessed very quickly. The applause was polite and friendly, but though Jenny was well liked by the other guests, and had elicited much sympathy with the injured foot, it was not as enthusiastic as it might have been.

When everybody had passed before the judges the manager of the hotel rose to announce the winners. Andrew's name was one of those called out, and amidst much clapping and cheering he went up to collect his prize—a bottle of wine. Ann, the receptionist, handed out the prizes. When Andrew took the bottle from her she put up her face for a kiss. There was much good-humoured laughing from the other guests as he bent down and lightly embraced her.

Afterwards, when the contest was over, Andrew asked a waiter to bring glasses. 'We're all going to sample my wine,' he announced.

At that moment Ann passed their group of chairs, and she paused and smiled. 'Using up your prize already?' To Jenny's ears there was something provocatively teasing about her tone.

'As you see.' Andrew grinned up at her. 'And you will sit down and join us, won't you?'

'Well . . .' She slanted an enigmatic look in Jenny's direction. 'Yes, thank you, I think I will.'

'That's the spirit!' Andrew was in good humour as he lifted the open bottle to his nose and pretended to sniff the bouquet with great thoughtfulness and consideration. 'Excellent,' he pronounced at last, with mock gravity.

'Worth the kiss?' Ann asked demurely.

'Absolutely.'

'You didn't mind, did you, Miss Windham?'
She had turned to Jenny.

'Of course not,' said Jenny, wondering why the
girl should make such an issue of the kiss, and at
the same time a little wary of the bright, hard voice.

'Should she have minded?' Andrew asked.

'Perhaps not.' Ann spoke in pretended uncer-
tainty. 'It's just . . . you and Miss Windham have
been spending so much time together. I thought
perhaps . . . On the other hand, there's the man
who . . .' She paused very deliberately. 'Oh, I *am*
sorry, Miss Windham. Perhaps I shouldn't have
said that. Perhaps Mr Langley doesn't know.'

'Know what?' Andrew asked quietly.

Ann was silent, waiting for Jenny to speak. 'What
Ann is trying to tell you,' Jenny said quietly, 'is that
I spent the day with Ross Sundy.' And as Andrew
wrinkled his brow at the mention of a name which
obviously meant nothing to him : 'Ross is a forester.
Don't you remember, Andrew, the man who helped
me down the mountain when I hurt my ankle?'

'Oh, that man,' Andrew said in a dismissing tone,
as if he did not take the matter at all seriously.
'You didn't tell me, Jenny.'

'I haven't had much chance to,' Jenny observed
quietly. 'We've all been very excited with the fancy-
dress, and after all, I only went out with him today.'

'I see.' Still there was no more than polite interest
in Andrew's voice. 'I didn't know you'd become so

99

friendly with him.'

'I haven't.' Jenny bit her lip, and wished she could stop the tell-tale colour from flooding her cheeks. 'He asked me to spend the day with him. We had a picnic. That's about all there was to it.'

'And yet I don't think he means quite so little to Miss Windham.' Ann was watching her closely, a dangerous look in her eyes. 'There was that kiss, after all, wasn't there, Miss Windham?'

'A kiss?' Andrew asked.

'Yes. That was why I didn't think Miss Windham would really mind if I kissed *you* just now,' Ann smiled. 'I mean, *our* kiss meant so little, didn't it?'

'And the kiss you saw meant no more.' Jenny's face was burning, as much from fury as from embarrassment. Why did this girl try so hard to make trouble?

'Well . . .' Ann said non-committally.

'What is this anyway?' Jenny said angrily. 'An inquisition? If I choose to kiss somebody that's entirely my business. But, since you saw it, you know it was no more than a peck. Why do you make it sound like a passionate embrace?'

'I suppose it wasn't really passionate,' Ann conceded reluctantly, 'but I don't know what preceded it. After all, the two of you were alone together all day.'

'I wish I knew what you were trying to get at,' Jenny demanded furiously. 'I decided to spend the day with Ross Sundy. Is there something wrong with that?'

'No.'

'And even if there was—what business is it of yours? I'm a guest here.'

'I know. It's just . . .' Ann looked down in pretended demureness. 'Perhaps I shouldn't say this— I can see how angry you are. But I'm really doing it only for your own good. You see, Mr Langley'— she turned to Andrew—'Ross Sundy has the reputation for being quite a ladies' man. A lot of girls who've been guests here could tell you that. Miss Windham—' she hesitated again, 'don't be taken in by that strong, silent forester's image.'

'I can look after myself,' Jenny said hotly.

'I wouldn't like you to fall in love with him. You're a nice girl, Miss Windham.' Jenny thought the word ' nice ' held a derogatory ring. 'I wouldn't like to see you hurt.'

'I don't think there's much danger of that,' Jenny said. 'That's the second time you've warned me. Perhaps we could change the subject now?'

'Yes,' Andrew said suddenly, stepping into the fray just as Ann was about to speak once more. Jenny mentally blessed him for his intervention. ' I think you've made the position pretty clear to Jenny. Now, ladies, I really think we should have the wine before the evening becomes too serious.'

Ann was wise enough to drop the subject after that. She did not sit with them for long, but while she was there she was very much the life and soul of the party. She could be very charming when she tried, Jenny found, and she soon had Andrew laughing at her anecdotes. In contrast, Jenny was very quiet. She sipped her wine and listened to the

101

scintillating wit that bounced between Andrew and Ann. Ross was not mentioned again, but Jenny felt that he had not been forgotten by any of them.

A little later, when Jenny got up to go, Andrew said he would walk with her to the bungalow. Mrs Ramsden was not with them. She had gone to bed soon after the judging was over.

Andrew linked his arm through hers, and as they walked through the darkness he recounted an incident that had occurred while he was out climbing that morning. They were at the door of the bungalow when the light-heartedness left his voice and he took her hand. 'Jenny,' he said, 'don't take what Ann said too seriously.'

'I won't,' she said quickly.

'Ann is a nice girl. I know she didn't mean to upset you.'

'I'm not upset.'

'Yes, you are. You've been upset since she joined us. Ann means well. As she said, she was only thinking of you.'

'Please, Andrew!'

'I can understand how it happened,' he went on. 'You're lonely during the day. Mrs Ramsden and my mom aren't suitable company for a lass like you. And there don't seem to be any unattached young people here at the moment. So if you did happen to meet up with the forester, that's no fault of yours.'

'Andrew . . .' If only she could stop him from going on, but her voice was thick with unshed tears.

102

'One of these days I'll take things a little easier and do a smaller walk with you. Would you like that, Jenny?'

She nodded wordlessly.

'Good night, my dear.' He drew her to him, and for the second time that day a man kissed her.

And then, mercifully, she was alone in the darkness of the bungalow. She undressed quickly, and slipped between the sheets, but in the moments before she fell asleep, like the shifting patterns in a kaleidoscope, the events of the day passed before her eyes.

# CHAPTER SEVEN

On a blue and golden morning a few days later
Ross came to her again. And as always Jenny's spirits
lifted at the sight of him.

'How's the foot getting on?' he enquired, squatting on his haunches beside her chair.

'I believe you're only interested in my foot,' she
said, laughing, resisting the temptation to reach
down and run her fingers through the curly hair.

'It's because it's so much a part of you that
I'm interested,' he rejoined. 'Let's see you walk.'
And when she had obliged: 'A great improvement.
I think it's good enough for what I have in mind.'

'And that is?' If only she could stop her heart
from leaping whenever he suggested any way in which
they could be together.

'Go and get a cardigan, and do whatever it is
that females must do before they go out. Then
come back to me.'

'Ross . . .' she began.

'Five minutes,' he said firmly, straightening and
going to a chair. 'That's all the time I'll give
you.'

Though she knew he was teasing she was back before the five minutes were over, having only paused to run a brush through her hair. A quick look in the mirror told her that her cheeks were flushed, and her eyes so bright that she needed no make-up. She found Mrs Ramsden, told her she was going out, and then hurried back to the garden.

'Good girl,' Ross said approvingly. 'Made it with thirty seconds to spare.'

'Where are we going, Ross?'

'I'll tell you in the car.' He had his hand through her arm as he guided her to the car-park. There were people in the garden and on the drive, but Jenny did not care. Fleetingly she thought of Ann's warning. But much as she might brood over the girl's words again later, nothing could destroy the happiness of the moment.

'Have you ever seen rock paintings?' Ross asked when they were turning from the hotel drive into the road.

'In books,' she told him.

'I mean the real thing. On the rocks themselves.'

'Oh, no.'

'I didn't think you had. I thought we'd have another picnic, Jenny. Afterwards I'll take you to see rock paintings.' He turned to her smiling. 'Or am I being too high-handed, just assuming that's what you would like to do?'

'No.' She smiled back at him. 'I'd love to do that.'

'Good.' He took a hand from the wheel and

reached out for one of hers. For a time they drove in silence, a contented silence which made conversation quite unnecessary. If Jenny had cared to she could have told him that she would have fallen in with just about any plan he might have suggested. To look at rock paintings would be fascinating, but all that really mattered was that she would be with him. This was the important thing, and Ann's nasty words could do nothing to change it.

The road they travelled on was one she had not seen before, and as always Jenny thrilled to the beauty and tranquillity of the countryside. Now and then she turned from the scenery to look as Ross. His profile was relaxed, his arms muscled and brown, the hand with which he guided the car expertly around the bends of the winding road was strong and confident. His other hand still held hers. Once when she looked at him he turned and smiled at her. He gave her hand a tiny squeeze. Then they came to a tricky part of the road, which required all his attention and skill, and he released her hand so that he could control the wheel more safely.

Deeper and deeper into the mountains they went. Once they drove along a narrow gully with the cliffs steep and close on either side. And then the road began to climb, and when they reached a plateau the view below them was dazzling.

'I enjoyed that,' Jenny said, when Ross stopped the car at last.

'I know.' He was smiling at her, a look of satisfaction in his eyes. 'I was watching you. You love beauty, don't you, Jenny?'

'Yes. It's all so lovely that I want to cry sometimes.'

'I feel that way too. People think one gets used to the mountains, but I never have. I don't think I ever will.' He paused, then asked, 'Could you get to like this type of life, Jenny?'

His eyes were so serious and compelling that she had to look away. What did his words mean? Was this just a casual question? Or was he testing her in some way? If only she knew the answer to that, then she would know too what to say.

'I think I could like it very much,' she said at last, quietly.

He did not speak. He just looked at her very quietly for a long moment, during which Jenny hardly breathed. Then he opened his door and came round to her side to help her out.

Once more they had their picnic beside the water, only this time it was just a stream, for they were now quite high in the mountains. The water danced between the rocks, so clear that every pebble could be seen. The sun shone down on the water, the light splintering the surface into a million diamonds.

As he had done before, Ross stood the bottles of fruit juice in the water to keep cool. Then he leaned back against a rock and closed his eyes.

Jenny watched him. He looked very tired, she thought. His face was deeply etched with lines and crevices, and now, in repose, it held an expression which touched at her heart. He was so still that she wondered if he had fallen asleep. But after a while he began to talk.

She had heard him talk in many different ways. There had been the mocking, hurtful tone, which she had come to dread, and the lighthearted banter which had them both laughing. There had been the disturbing tenderness which had haunted her dreams. And on their last outing there had been the seriousness with which he had told her about the forests and his work. Once more he was talking about the forests, but this time his tone and his words held a depth she had not heard before. He spoke not only of his work, but told her his dreams and ambitions for the future. Then he asked her about herself. After a time they began to talk about other things, of music, and of books they had both read. To anyone listening, Jenny thought, their conversation would have seemed strange, as if they touched on topics not normally discussed in such surroundings between a forester and a young girl. Yet their conversation was not strange at all. And Jenny had never felt closer to Ross.

It was quiet up here in the mountains, so far from any sign of life. There was only the sound of the leaping water, the rustle of the long grass in the wind, the call of birds far above them. The sun grew warmer, and Jenny revelled in the touch of it on her skin. She thought she had never known such peace, such tranquillity. They could have been a million miles away from civilization.

Later, when the sun stood high above them, Ross unpacked the haversack and they began to eat. The lunch he had brought was, as before, simple and quite delicious. When they had cleared away the debris, he said, 'Now I'm going to show you the paintings.'

He led the way over rocks and boulders, turning to give her a hand whenever the going became steep or a little rough. Her ankle was so much stronger now that she was able to manage quite well. Sometimes, as she had done before, when they came to parts that were sloping but not rough, Jenny sat down and just slid to the bottom, while Ross wached her and grinned.

Presently they came to a pile of rocks that looked a little different. Jenny saw that they formed the entrance to a small cave. 'We're here.' Ross turned and took her hand.

Though she had known more or less what to expect, the sight that met her eyes left her dumbfounded. In books, pictures of rock paintings had seemed flat and a little colourless. Now, seeing them on these rocks, she was amazed at how realistic they really were—pictures of men, of animals, and of hunters, beautifully painted, in colours that had stood up to the ravages of wind and rain and time. Pictures that depicted the lives of men who had once roamed these mountains hundreds, perhaps thousands of years ago. Men who had struggled to eke out an existence from these bare cliffs, who had lived on the animals they could hunt, and on berries and roots that grew from the soil; who had slaked their thirst in the cool water of the mountain streams. Men who had fought a constant battle to exist, and who yet had had time to express the beauty that existed around them, as well as the longings that dwelt within their souls.

Jenny needed time to assimilate the different impressions the rock paintings evoked in her. At last she said, 'I never dreamed it would be so interesting.'

'I could lend you some books . . .' Ross said tentatively.

'Oh, yes!' She turned to him wonderingly, thinking how little she really knew of this strange, disturbing man, and how much she wanted to know more. 'Is this another of your interests, Ross?'

'I find it very absorbing,' he said quietly.

They spent some time in the little cave, and Jenny touched the bare rock and studied the paintings, marvelling at the accurate lines of the angular drawings, and the colours that must have been mixed from mud and berries and roots.

At last Ross said, 'It's getting late. I think we must be going, Jenny.'

They began to climb back with Ross leading the way. All was well till Jenny came to a pile of rocks that she could not negotiate. Despairingly she looked at the rugged expanse above her, trying to find a way of getting to the top of it. Finally she called, 'Ross!'

'Jenny?' He looked around questioningly.

'I'm stuck!'

'Good heavens!' He grinned suddenly. 'Whatever was I thinking of! Even without an injured foot you'd have trouble getting up there.' With a few quick bounds he was beside her. Somehow, with his help, Jenny managed to get up the steep incline.

But the climb had tired her more than she realised. Ross looked at her and must have seen the strain and the weariness, for all at once he bent and lifted her in his arms.

'This is becoming a habit,' she said shakily.

'A very nice habit.' He laughed softly as he carried her. 'Little Jenny—what have I done to you?'

He carried her a long way, much further than was necessary. It was as if, all at once, he was loth to put her down.

At last he stopped and lowered her gently to the ground. Then he put his arms around her. She looked up at him, and her heart lurched at the expression in his eyes. He bent his head, and then his lips were on hers, and he was kissing her, gently at first and then with a sudden hardness.

When he released her she was trembling. 'Jenny . . .' There was a look in his eyes which she could not understand. 'Jenny, you're so lovely, but so vulnerable. I don't want to hurt you.' And as she shook her head wordlessly, unable to speak because of the tears stinging her throat, he took up the haversack and led her back to the car.

Once again they were silent on the drive back to the hotel, but this time the silence was more poignant. Jenny's thoughts were in a turmoil, and whenever she felt herself unobserved she would try to steal a glance at his face. What did he feel? What did he think?

'Little Jenny,' he had called her. There had been such a wealth of tenderness in his voice. Was this

111

what Ann meant when she said Ross was a ladies' man—that he liked all pretty girls and ended up breaking their hearts? It could not be. It just could not.

They were nearly at the hotel when Ross stopped the car at a look-out point. In silence they sat looking down at the vista of slopes and valleys, painted now with the shadows of late afternoon. Presently he said, 'I won't be seeing you for a while, Jenny.'

'Oh!' She turned to him quickly, the happiness fading within her.

'I have to go on a trip, speak to the men in some of the other districts.' He took her hand and stroked it gently. 'I just thought I'd tell you.'

'How long will you be away?'

'I'm not certain. At least ten days.' He looked at her quietly, his hand still stroking hers. 'Jenny . . .' he began, then stopped, having decided apparently not to go on with what he had been about to say. Abruptly he started the car, and drove the last miles back to the hotel.

When he had gone Jenny went to tell Mrs Ramsden she was back. Then she went down to the river. The broad rock where she had sat that first afternoon had become her favourite spot. She went there whenever she felt the need of solitude, or when she wanted to think. At this moment she needed to be alone. She did not want to speak to anyone and risk the preciousness of the day being spoiled.

Almost without moving she sat on her rock,

gazing into the mountains, and reliving the day she had spent. She remembered the tenderness she had glimpsed in Ross's eyes. She remembered how he had kissed her.

And then, quite involuntarily, her mind went back to the words that Ann had spoken. Perhaps Ross was really just a very good actor, a man who could make every girl feel that she was special. But if he was not an actor . . . ? Her mind could not cope with the implications of what that would mean. For if by some chance he had fallen in love with her, as she had with him, what future could there be for them? If she married him it would mean living in the forests of Africa. How far she would be from England and the life she knew so well, a distance measured not only in miles. A girl would have to be very much in love to take such a step—as Jenny was indeed in love. She knew it now. She could take that step—but would he ask her?

The setting sun painted the sky with vivid colours and the mountain peaks were aflame with a translucence that was dazzling. At her feet the river bubbled and tumbled, its never-ending song creating a music she knew she could never grow tired of. From somewhere in the distance came the sounds of a cowbell and the shouts of a herdboy as he led his herd back to a distant farm.

Jenny's eyes blurred with sudden tears. She did not even know whether her tears were for the beauty all around her, or for the love which had grown into something greater than she had ever known.

# CHAPTER EIGHT

The next few days were curious ones. Jenny went about in a state that was not unlike a trance. She spoke to people, she laughed, responded to jokes, did all the social and conventional things that were expected of her. And all the while, inside her, she was living out a different world, a world of the emotions that was hidden from all who came into contact with her.

Again and again she relived the time she had spent with Ross. In terms of actual hours this was not much, but these hours had been packed with such contrasting emotions. She would think of Ross trundling her in the wheelbarrow, and let out an involuntary laugh. She would remember the times he had lifted her into his arms and carried her. She could still feel the harness of his chest, and the strength of his arms: could still smell the composite scent of maleness. The touch of his hand upon hers was real, as was the tenderness in his eyes. Again and again she could hear his voice whisper 'Little Jenny,' and feel the passion contained in the lips that had pressed down upon

114

hers.

He had not said how long he would be away. He had seemed certain it would be at least ten days. Jenny did not mind. For she knew she would see him when he returned.

How this would come about she did not know. Perhaps he would come to the hotel to look for her, or perhaps she would meet him in the forests. But she would see him—she had no doubt of that.

In the meantime, there was a certain restfulness in the knowledge that he was away. For she needed time to think and to sort out her emotions.

At night, when she retired to the bungalow, she found it difficult to sleep. Long after the room was in darkness, and Mrs Ramsden had fallen asleep, Jenny would stand at the window, looking out at the star-studded sky and the black silhouettes that were the mountain. She was beginning to think of them as *her* mountain. Her mountains. Her forest. Her rivers.

And then she would pull herself up sharply. What if Ross did not love her; if Ross said nothing to make her stay? Then, when the time came for Mrs Ramsden to go back to England, Jenny too would have to catch a plane and go back home. The mountains and the forests and the rivers, all these would become no more than a memory.

And Ross . . . From somewhere within her she would have to find the strength to say goodbye to Ross, to take her leave of him without showing that her heart was breaking.

Jenny was still spending a lot of time with Mrs

Ramsden and Mrs Langley in the garden. Though her ankle was so much better now she found that long walks still tired her, and that if she climbed or walked too far her foot would start to ache.

Often she walked down to the river. She loved the hours spent on the broad rock by the river, sometimes with a book, and sometimes just gazing into the mountains.

After the day when she had discussed Ross with her, and had expressed the hope that Jenny was not falling in love with him, Mrs Ramsden did not mention him often. When she did it was only casually, but Jenny would look up sometimes and find the other woman's eyes upon her face, thoughtful and a little concerned. Jenny knew Mrs Ramsden still hoped she might have a future with Andrew, but she was grateful to her for not making her talk about her feelings.

Then there was Andrew. Jenny thought sometimes that Andrew's attitude had changed a little, though in what way she could not have said. He was as friendly as ever, but sometimes in the evening, when they were playing Scrabble or Monopoly and she would be puzzling over her next move, she would look up unexpectedly and find his eyes upon her. His expression would be enigmatic. When he saw her that expression would vanish, and the easygoing smile take its place. But she knew the look had been there. What was Andrew thinking? Had Ann's troublemaking struck harder than Jenny had imagined?

And then, one evening, when the weather was

unusually warm, Andrew stretched his legs restlessly beside the log fire. 'I'm going for a walk, Jenny,' he said, getting to his feet. 'Will you come with me?'

'In the dark?'

'There's a full moon. You'll be able to see.'

She hesitated a moment. Then she said, 'All right.' As she walked out of the room with Andrew she turned and looked back. Mrs Ramsden and Mrs Langley were watching them, their faces hopeful and expectant. Jenny felt momentarily irritated, then she told herself she was being silly.

It was a lovely starlit night, and the air had a crispness that was exhilarating. Andrew took her hand and they walked slowly through the garden. Beneath some pines they stopped. Jenny found herself edged back against a tree, so that when Andrew spoke she had to lift her head to look at him. 'Jenny . . .' His voice had lost its usual gay exuberance.

She looked up at him and saw that his eyes were brilliant in the moonlight. 'What is it, Andrew?' She forced herself to speak casually.

'You're very beautiful. Did you know?'

'Andrew . . .' she began.

'You do know, don't you?'

'Please . . .' Her voice was pleading. 'What is this?'

'I want to kiss you.' He had put his hands on her shoulders and was drawing her to him.

'No!' she exclaimed.

'Why not?' He was very close to her now. 'I'm a man and you're a woman—and we like each

117

other.'

'No, please!' She felt a little sick.

'What's a kiss between friends?' He bent towards her, tilted her chin and pressed his lips to hers. After a moment, when he found her completely unresponsive, he straightened.

'I'm sorry,' she whispered.

He did not answer. They walked on slowly. Andrew fumbled in his pocket for his pipe and began to fill it with tobacco. He began to draw on it, and Jenny had the feeling that the action steadied him.

Finally he spoke. 'You can't tell me you've not been kissed before.' He sounded angry.

'Andrew, please!'

'Andrew, please,' he mocked her. 'What was it that Ann said that day, Jenny?'

'Ann . . .?' She felt herself trembling.

'About the forester? She said you'd kissed him.'

'He kissed me,' she said quietly. 'And it wasn't even a kiss, just a peck.'

'Really?'

'Ann—likes to dramatise.' She was growing angry. Why should she have to even try to justify her behaviour?

'I'm beginning to wonder.' Andrew stopped, then said evenly, 'Is Ross Sundy the reason you don't want me to kiss you?'

'Of course not! He has nothing to do with it!' She knew she spoke a little too vehemently, but could not help herself. 'Andrew, I'm cold. Please let's go back inside.'

118

'Very well.' He gave a bitter laugh. 'Let's go back and play parlour games. What shall it be, Jenny? Monopoly—or Scrabble?'

She did not answer, and soon after they had returned to the lounge he excused himself and left the room.

Later, when Jenny and Mrs Ramsden walked back to their bungalow they came past the little card-room, and Jenny heard voices. One she knew was Andrew's. The other? There was a sudden burst of laughter, and Jenny recognised the voice. It was Ann.

Mrs Ramsden cast a quick look at her. Though she had asked no questions, it must have been obvious when Jenny and Andrew returned from their walk that something had happened. She too had recognised the voices and was obviously wondering whether Jenny minded.

For no rational reason Jenny felt a little angry. She was not jealous of Andrew. After all, she could have let him kiss her if she had wanted to. What she resented was that he was making a point of being with the other girl just because she, Jenny, had refused to kiss him. It was almost as if he were trying to humiliate her in return for what he had considered a humiliation.

And then Jenny thought of Ross, and all at once everything else was quite meaningless.

All next day she dreaded the evening that lay ahead, wondering how Andrew would behave. Yet she need not have worried. Andrew seemed to have regained his good humour. They played a card game,

119

laughing and talking, as if nothing had happened. The kiss was not mentioned between them.

At the end of the evening, when they were putting the cards away and getting ready to go back to the bungalow, Andrew said, 'Looking forward to the dance tomorrow night, Jenny?'

She looked up quickly, wondering what was coming.

'Didn't you see the bulletin board?' he asked.

'Yes, yes, I did.'

'We'll go together, Jenny?'

'Yes.' Fleetingly she thought of Ross, wishing he would be there, knowing he wouldn't be, for the ten days were not yet over. 'Thanks, Andrew,' she smiled. 'It should be fun.'

'So Ann says.' She wished he wouldn't keep mentioning the other girl's name, for it grated on her nerves. She wondered too at the odd look in his eyes. 'It will be a nice change from Monopoly,' Andrew said dryly.

Jenny took things easy the next day, so that she would be able to enjoy the evening. Her irritation of the day before had been overcome. She found she was actually looking forward to the dance. She had grown accustomed to the evenings in front of the fire, and there had been so little time for dancing and parties in the last few years. It should not matter that it was not Ross with whom she would be dancing. What mattered was that she would laugh and dance and spend a lovely evening, and while Andrew could never be Ross, he was neverless very good company and fun to be with.

A little while before supper she went to the bungalow. She had brought only one evening dress with her, and now she took it from the cupboard. It was a pretty dress with a swirling skirt beneath a close-fitting bodice and a scooped-out neck. It was a deep shade of pink which enhanced the delicate colour of her cheeks.

After she had bathed, she dressed, dashed a few drops of perfume behind her ears and on her wrists, and clipped on ear-rings of white and gold.

When she was ready she went to the mirror and looked at herself. The sun had turned her face and arms to a honey-gold colour that emphasised the fairness of her hair and deepened the colour of her cheeks and eyes. Her hair had been bleached by the sun, so that it was fairer than ever, with golden highlights streaking through it. She had spent some time brushing it, and now it fell to her shoulders, loose and smooth and swinging.

She wished that Ross could see her now. The only clothes he had seen her in were slacks and shirts, spruce and smart enough for walking through the forests, but her reflection told her that tonight she looked different. Without being vain, she knew she had never before looked so pretty.

On their way to the dining-room, Mrs Ramsden and Jenny had to walk past the reception, where Ann was leaning over the visitors' book. After supper, Jenny knew, Ann would join in the merrymaking, for she would be free by then, but now she was still on duty.

'Hello, Miss Windham.' The girl had looked up

121

and now she was smiling at her, so that Jenny was forced to stop a moment. 'What a pretty dress!'

'Thank you. You look lovely too.' Jenny had reluctantly to admit that Ann looked stunning. The glossy dark hair had been brushed into a flattering style, and she wore a dress of vivid emerald which accentuated her flamboyant loveliness.

'Why, thank you.' There was an enigmatic look in the other girl's eyes, Jenny thought, then chided herself for thinking it. Perhaps it was not Ann's fault that she could not rid herself of the dislike she felt for her.

'I suppose you'll be going to the dance with Mr Langley?' Ann asked as Jenny was about to walk on.

Jenny looked at her quietly for a moment, without answering, a little taken aback at the girl's presumptuousness.

'We'll be sitting together,' she said.

'That's what I thought.' Ann threw her a dazzling smile, and once again Jenny wondered why she dreamed there was malice in it. 'Have a super time.'

'Thank you. You too.'

'What a nice girl she is,' Mrs Ramsden commented as they walked on.

'Yes . . .' Jenny looked quickly at the older woman, wondering if she was being sarcastic, but her face was serene and open.

'Always so ready to help. So obliging. Pretty too.' Mrs Ramsden threw her a look. 'I really think she would like to be friends with you, Jenny.'

'You really think that?' Jenny asked quietly.

'She seems to go out of her way to talk to you,

and always so nicely. Why, Jenny, look how friendly she was just now—complimenting you on your dress, and hoping you'd have a good time.'

' . . . Yes.' She could not tell Mrs Ramsden that she had felt the other girl had been wishing her dead while she was mouthing the niceties.

'Why don't you give her a chance, Jenny? It must be a lonely life here at the hotel. Perhaps you could spend some time together when she has a free afternoon.' Mrs Ramsden must have seen the horror on Jenny's face, for she looked distressed, then said, 'Of course, I don't want to foist anything on to you. I just thought . . . Well, you're both young. You must have things in common.'

'I . . .' Jenny began.

'I know . . .' Mrs Ramsden hesitated, then went on, 'I know you like to spend time with Mr Sundy. But he's usually busy with his forestry duties, isn't he? And Andrew . . . Andrew is away on the mountains most days.'

'Yes, well, perhaps . . . Look, Mrs Ramsden,' said Jenny, desperate to change the subject, 'there are Mrs Langley and Andrew. They look as if they're waiting for us. Shall we go and say hello?'

The look in the eyes of Mrs Langley and Andrew when they saw Jenny confirmed how lovely she looked, and somehow their approval added an extra glow to her eyes and brought spots of colour to her cheeks. 'Looking forward to the evening?' Andrew asked, taking her hand.

'Yes. Oh, Andrew, we'll have fun!' She felt light-hearted and gay.

'We will.' Andrew turned to Mrs Ramsden. 'People are joining up for dinner tonight. I asked the waiter to put you and Jenny at our table. Is that all right?'

'Yes, of course,' Mrs Ramsden said warmly, while Jenny wondered why they had not been consulted about this first. Then she realised how silly she was being. The four of them had grown so close in the time they had been here that it was only natural that they should sit together tonight. Besides, she told herself, nothing was going to spoil the fun that lay ahead. 'I think that's a lovely idea,' she said, smiling as she added her comment to Mrs Ramsden's.

The meal was delicious, and Andrew ordered a bottle of wine, which immediately added a festive note to the evening. The table began to ring with laughter. Andrew told jokes which they had not heard before, and Mrs Ramsden topped them with ones of her own. Jenny had one glass of wine, and then another. The golden liquid warmed and relaxed her, and she began to feel so lighthearted that even the ridiculous feelings of dread and insecurity induced by the receptionist were dispelled.

When the meal was over, Jenny and Andrew left the two older women in the lounge and walked to the little night-club which the hotel kept for their dances.

'Isn't it pretty!' Jenny exclaimed as they entered the room which was already noisy with laughter and high spirits. Balloons in bright bunches hung from the walls. Wine-bottles with candles in them stood on the tables. Streamers and paper flowers were everywhere, giving the room a party atmosphere. A three-piece band had travelled from town for the evening, and they were busy setting up their intruments on a dais beside the dance floor.

The night-club was beginning to fill up, and Jenny saw that many of the guests had made up parties. Honeymooners had gathered at one table, young and old married couples were at others. There was even a table of cheerful teenagers. Men were lighting the table-top candles, and the women were colourful in their pretty dresses.

They found a table in a corner, and Jenny gazed about her entranced. 'You look like a girl at her first dance,' Andrew commented, as he struck a match and leaned forward to light the taper.

'Do you know,' she said a little wistfully, 'in a way it's just how I feel.'

'You must have gone to dances in England?' He looked at her curiously as he shook out the match and dropped it into the ashtray.

'Oh, I did, but ages ago. It's so long since I danced, Andrew. This kind of thing—dancing and music and pretty dresses—it's as if it's part of another world.'

'I'm sorry, I should have realised . . .' He reached for her hand and kept it in his. After a moment she decided to let him hold it. He smiled at her. 'We're going to enjoy ourselves, Jenny.'

'I know that,' she said, as the band struck up a lively tune that set her heels tapping on the floor beneath the table. Amid much clapping and cheering one of the honeymoon couples took the floor.

Moments later they were joined by another couple, and then another. Andrew rose from his chair, and with the hand that was still holding hers, he drew her to her feet.

They stepped on to the dance floor, and he put his arm around her. Jenny was delighted with the ease with which they danced together. 'You're as light as a feather,' he complimented her.

'You make it so easy to follow,' she smiled up to him.

After a few dances the music became wild and the beat furious. 'I can't,' Jenny mouthed at Andrew. 'My foot . . .'

'I know.' He was shouting through the noise. 'We'll stand out and watch this one.'

For a while they stood at the side and watched, and clapped to the beat. Then the music became quiet and dreamy. Men and women moved back from the separateness of the wilder dances and came into each other's arms, and Jenny and Andrew went back on to the floor.

Andrew's arm was close about her. His chin touched her hair. The feeling of well-being induced by the wine was still with her, and as Jenny let herself drift about the dance-floor, watching the gliding figures all around her, she felt a little as if she were in a dream.

Out of the corner of her eye she saw Ann, dancing with a tall thin man. So well disposed did she feel towards all and sundry at the moment that for once she regarded the other girl quite amiably. Ann and her partner danced nearer. They turned, and then Ann's back was towards her, and the man she was dancing with was facing her. Jenny grew rigid with shock. Ross! Ann was dancing with Ross!

Without thinking she stood quite still, so that Andrew stumbled against her. 'What the . . .' he muttered. Then, as he saw her shock, he turned his head, and his eyes followed her gaze, and she felt him stiffen. For what seemed a long moment but could have been no more than seconds, Ross and Jenny looked at each other, and Andrew stood watching them both. Then they were dancing again, and Andrew was propelling her with the strength of his arms, for she did not have the will to make her numb legs move.

Quite suddenly, catching Jenny totally unprepared, Andrew pulled her closer and pressed his lips down hard upon hers. So numb was she at that moment that she stood quite still, unprotesting, with his arms like two bands of steel about her, as he kissed her. By the time she had summoned the strength to push him away, the kiss had ended. She was too close to Andrew to see his face, but as she lifted her head Ross was staring at her. His face was a frozen mask of hurt and anger.

She looked at him pleadingly, desperately, wanting to reach out and touch him, to call to him that the kiss was not of her doing, that Andrew, who had kissed her only once before, must have done this to make him jealous. But even if she had been able to reach him, she could not have spoken, for her mouth had gone dry with a dryness that did not permit speech. And the pleading in her eyes went unheeded, for the look in his face did not change.

She became conscious of Ann. Ann too was watching her. Her eyes were mocking and satisfied. Even as Jenny watched, the girl's arm went up around Ross's neck, and her head came to rest against his shoulder.

Jenny was quite oblivious of the other people on the dance floor. For those terrible moments it seemed as if there were just four people, frozen in an awful nightmare. The music quickened, and the crowds around them began to shift. Moments later, as Andrew guided her one way, and Ross and Ann danced another, the two couples had become parted. She could no longer see Ross's face. All she saw was the bare arm that curled around his neck.

'Why did you do it?' She had found her speech at last. Andrew was humming to the music, and did not answer.

'Andrew!' She beat her hand against his chest. 'Why did you do it?'

'Do what?' He was looking down at her, his eyes glimmering with amusement.

'Why did you kiss me like that?'

'Because I like you, sweetheart,' he said, as indulgently as if he were talking to a child.

'But at that moment!'

'Was that moment different from any other?'

'You know it was.'

'Well, let me see.' He pretended to think. 'Perhaps it was that the music was soft and you were just so sweet in my arms. I told you once before that you were pretty. Remember?'

She did not answer him. He was not going to admit he had done it to make Ross jealous, but he had. She was as sure of that as she had ever been sure of anything in her life.

So many evenings they had spent together, she and Andrew, and yet before he had heard of Ross it had never occurred to him to kiss her. There had been something almost brotherly in his attitude to her, in the companionable hours spent beside the fire. She was certain that Andrew had never thought of her as anything more than a good companion. But her interest in Ross had piqued him, and hurt him in some domain of his male pride. In return he had tried to hurt her, and Ross, as best as he could.

The music ended and the band stopped to rest. Still humming, Andrew led her back to their table. The candle was no longer burning, and Jenny was glad of the healing darkness, glad that she could sit where nobody would see her. Tears stung her eyes and she was bending down to take a tissue from her bag, when she heard the voice, and looked up quickly.

'May we join you?' It was Ann. She stood by their table, her hand in Ross's. Ross looked reluctant. He muttered something and tried to walk on, but Ann tugged at his hand and made him stay. Her smile was cold and radiant, as Andrew said, 'Of course. Please do.'

'I really don't think . . .' Ross was protesting, but Ann was already pulling out a chair.

'There are no other free tables, darling,' she said as she sat down. 'Andrew and Jenny won't mind.

We're all friends.'

Ross had no option but to sit. Ann began to make the introductions. 'You know Jenny Windham, of course. And this'—again the radiant smile—'is Jenny's friend Andrew Langley. Andrew—Ross Sundy.' It was all done with such incredible poise and ease, the atmosphere of the night-club lending itself to the dropping of surnames.

'Andrew . . .' Ann leaned forward coquettishly, 'do you and Jenny particularly want to sit in the dark? Perhaps we could light this candle?'

'Oh, no . . .' Jenny began in alarm. They were the first words she had uttered, but she knew she could not endure the flickering light of the candle on her face at this moment.

'Nobody will object if you and Andrew want to hold hands under the table,' Ann said in honeyed tones, and laughed provocatively. 'Well, Andrew?'

'Sure, honey.' Andrew struck a match, and moments later the flickering glow of the candle lit up the four faces around the table.

Talk and laughter gained momentum in all corners of the night-club. Their table was no exception. Ann could talk amusingly and well, as Jenny already knew. Soon she and Andrew were keeping up a flow of repartee that was slick and sophisticated, and must have been very funny, for though Jenny could not see the humour, Ann and Andrew laughed uproariously after each sally. She noticed that Ross too seemed unamused, for he was silent.

'So quiet, Jenny?' Ann commented once. 'Andrew, give the girl a chance to talk, will you?' They were all looking at her now, and Jenny forced herself to smile and say, 'I suppose I just enjoy listening.'

'Ah, the good listener,' commented Ann. Perhaps it was the expression on her face that made it so, but for some reason this remark too seemed to be incredibly funny.

Jenny sat stiffly through the talk and the cigarette smoke and the flickering light of the candle. Her eyes were burning and her head ached. She still felt as if she were in the throes of a nightmare. If only she could wake up and find herself in the blessed darkness of the bungalow. Once or twice she ventured a glance at Ross, but he would not meet her eyes. Ann's chair was close to his, her arm lay across his lap, and every now and then she would glance at him and stroke his cheek with an air that spoke of long intimacy and familiarity.

Presently the music started again. Andrew asked Jenny to dance. He held her very tightly, and she did not have the strength to push him away. In any event, it hardly seemed to matter any more.

When the band paused to rest they returned to their table. Andrew drew his chair close to Jenny's and put his arm around her. Ann leaned her head against Ross's shoulder. And still the barbed jokes flew, fast and furious.

Again the band began to play. Ross turned to Jenny, and addressing himself to her for the first time that evening, asked if she would dance with him. She had a moment of panic. It was what she wanted more than anything else. But not here, not now. Not in these circumstances. She could not dance with Ross when Andrew and Ann would watch them with such knowingness.

'Well, Jenny?' Ross was standing now, his eyes cold, his face waiting.

'Yes . . . yes, of course.' She did not know how she willed her numb limbs to rise and to make the expected movements.

He led her on to the dance floor, and held out his arms to her. For a while they danced in silence. He held her very correctly, one arm around her waist, the other hand holding hers, making no movement to draw her to him, and though she could not feel his body against hers, she could sense the stiffness that was in him.

'I thought for a moment that you didn't want to dance with me,' he said at last, breaking the silence.

'Oh, no, it wasn't you . . .' She was stammering, wildly seeking an excuse. 'My foot. Just that my foot . . .'

'I noticed your foot was fine when you were dancing with Andrew Langley,' he said woodenly.

'Ross . . .' She looked at him pleadingly. 'Ross, I . . . When did you get back?'

'Yesterday.'

'Oh! I thought you were going to be away much longer.'

'I came back earlier because I wanted to be at this dance with you.' The words were spoken evenly, with no expression whatsoever. Jenny's head jerked up quickly, but his eyes were fixed on some distant point.

132

'I . . . I didn't know. Oh, Ross,' she said with a sudden break in her voice, 'I didn't know.'

'But I left a message for you.'

'You did?' she said urgently. 'When, Ross? Where?'

'I came to the hotel, but you were out. I asked Ann to tell you.'

'But . . .' She shook her head numbly. 'Ross . . .'

'You were going to the dance with Andrew Langley.'

'Oh, no!'

'When I came down here to find you tonight Ann told me. She came with me instead.'

'But, Ross,' Jenny protested, 'that's not the way it was.'

'You did tell Ann you were coming with Andrew?'

'Yes. Yes, I did. But, Ross, you don't understand. You see . . .'

'I understand only too well,' he interrupted her. He was looking into her face now, and his eyes were cold. 'Andrew is good fun. You get on well with him. Ann told me about your relationship with him.'

'Relationship?' she echoed.

'You spend all your evenings together. You do, don't you?'

Jenny nodded silently. There was a hard lump in her throat, and she was trying so hard not to cry that it was quite useless even to attempt to speak, and to explain that the whole implication of his words was all wrong.

'During the day Andrew is out climbing,' Ross

133

went on relentlessly, 'training for his great expedition. That leaves you to your own devices. That's why, during the day, you don't mind being with me.'

'No, Ross!'

'No, Ross!' he copied her mockingly. 'Yes, Ross. Oh, Jenny, don't you think I know how it is? Didn't I see it all myself? The way Andrew kissed you? No man kisses a girl with such passion, in the middle of a crowded dance floor, unless he's used to kissing that girl.'

'Ross,' she said very quietly, with some semblance of control over her voice, 'Andrew was the one who did the kissing.'

'I didn't see you struggle very hard to stop him.' He looked down at her, a bitter smile tugging at his lips. 'I thought you were different, Jenny, but you're not! You're like all the other flirts I've met in my life. How many men do you have to your string? Andrew and me—and Neil Donaldson . . . And how many others?'

'You're not being fair,' she said furiously, snatching her hand from him and dabbing at a treacherous tear.

'No?' He pulled her suddenly close. 'Look, Jenny. Andrew and Ann are dancing together. They're both watching us. Shall I kiss you now, my dear, the way you were kissed by him?'

'Don't you dare!' she burst out violently.

'No.' He relaxed his hold so abruptly that she nearly fell. 'I won't kiss you. Not because I wouldn't dare. Just . . . just because I've lost all desire to.'

The evening ended at last. Outside the little nightclub they said their goodnights. Ann had her arm around Ross's waist; his arm lay across her shoulders. Andrew held Jenny's hand. 'Jenny's cold,' he said. 'Look, she's shivering. Goodnight, folks. I'm going to walk this little girl to her bungalow.'

'Goodnight, Jenny, Andrew . . .' Ann reached up suddenly and kissed Andrew's cheek. 'Super evening, wasn't it?' Then she and Ross wandered off together into the darkness.

Andrew and Jenny watched them go, then Andrew led her to her bungalow. 'Goodnight, sweetheart.' He put his arms around her, kissed her again, mockingly and hard, just as he had done on the dancefloor. Then he released her abruptly and walked away.

When she closed the door of the bungalow Jenny was trembling. She did not switch on the light. She just leaned against the door, feeling sick and drained and very tired. She lay down on her bed, wanting only to cry. But the tears did not come.

She got to her feet and went to stand at the window. Above her was the star-filled sky. There were stars she recognised from English skies, but there were other stars as well—the stars of the Southern Hemisphere which she had not known in England.

With what high hopes she had left there. She had been looking forward to this holiday, to mountains and rivers and sun and rest. Little had she thought that love would enter her life, that she would meet a man whom she would love so much that the idea of spending her life without him would be unbearable.

Perhaps she would tell Mrs Ramsden that she wanted to go home. The older woman seemed quite recovered from her illness. More than ever lately Jenny wondered whether Lynn had not asked her to go with her mother, not so much because Mrs Ramsden needed a companion, but because she wanted Jenny to get away and have a change.

Of course, Mrs Ramsden was shrewd. She would guess why Jenny wanted to leave the mountains. Jenny did not know if she could bear to see the pity that would be in the other woman's eyes. But far worse was the thought of remaining here.

A picture came to Jenny of the village—of the cottage with the honeysuckle and the climbing roses, and the memories of her parents. Suddenly she was swept with a violent wave of longing and homesickness.

It was then that the tears came. She threw herself on to her bed, and in the darkness of the little bungalow, beneath the star-studded African sky so very far from home, Jenny cried until she could cry no more.

# CHAPTER NINE

'Jenny!' A thin voice woke her. Jenny opened her eyes and saw that the sun was already so high in the sky that it was filtering through the curtains and making a pattern on the carpet. 'Jenny!' She heard it again.

'Mrs Ramsden?' Jenny rubbed her eyes and looked across to the other bed where the older woman lay. The voice had lacked its usual strength and cheerfulness, and now she saw that the face on the pillow was pale and tired.

Jenny got quickly out of bed and went over to her. 'I'm sorry, I overslept,' she said remorsefully.

'The dance lost night . . . I wouldn't have woken you . . .'

'You're not well!' Jenny exclaimed.

'No. I'm afraid I'm having one of my bad spells.'

'You'll be all right,' Jenny said reassuringly. Lynn had told her what to do if her mother became ill. 'I'll get dressed quickly, then I'll go up to the office and phone the doctor.'

'Thank you, dear.' Mrs Ramsden managed a

wan smile.

Jenny pulled on a few clothes. She cast a perfunctory look at her pale face in the mirror as she tugged a brush through her rumpled hair. 'I'll be right back,' she smiled at Mrs Ramsden as she went to the door.

Ann was already at the desk when Jenny came to the office. The girl was as poised as always, sleek and cool and pretty. Obviously the lateness of the night before had not robbed her of her beauty sleep. Jenny was aware of the appraising eyes on her own dishevelled appearance.

'I'd like to use the phone, please,' she said. 'Mrs Ramsden isn't well. How do I go about calling the doctor?'

'I have his number right here.' Ann opened a file and gave the number to Jenny. 'The old lady's not too bad, I hope?'

'I don't think so. But she needs attention.'

Jenny dialled the number. There was an engaged signal, and she replaced the receiver.

'Did you enjoy the dance?' Ann's expression was so friendly and open that Jenny wondered if she was the only one to suspect the guile that lay beneath the surface.

'Very much, thank you.' Not for the world would she have admitted how unhappy she had been.

'Yes, it was fun.' Ann smiled a secret smile, and Jenny wondered involuntarily what had happened between her and Ross after they had all said goodnight. But the thought that came into her mind was so unbearable that she thrust it quickly away again.

She dialled the number once more. It was still engaged. In the meantime, there was something that did need saying. 'Ann,' she looked at the other girl levelly, 'why didn't you give me Ross's message?'

'Message?' Ann's eyes were too wide.

'Ross asked you to tell me that he would be here last night—that he wanted me to be with him.'

'Oh, that!' Ann lifted her shoulders carelessly, but there was a wary look in her eyes. 'But I did begin to tell you.'

'Really?' Jenny said coolly. 'I don't remember it. In fact, I don't remember any mention of Ross's name.'

'I asked if you were going to be with Andrew Langley.'

'Yes . . .' Jenny said slowly.

'You said you were.'

'You made it sound like a casual question.'

'Oh, heavens!' Ann said impatiently. 'Such an issue!'

'You didn't mention Ross's message at all.'

'Perhaps I didn't. What of it?'

'I want to know the reason,' Jenny said evenly.

'I was only thinking of you, how embarrassing it would have been if you'd had two escorts. After all, you'd already agreed to go with Andrew, so you could hardly have put him off.'

'You could have let me make my own decision,' Jenny said. Ann was so adept at twisting situations to suit herself that there was no point in taking the matter any further. In any event, the damage had been done.

139

She picked up the receiver again, and this time there was a ringing tone. She spoke to the doctor's nurse and left a message for the doctor to call. When she turned again she saw that Ann was now busy over her books. The glossy black hair fell forward over her face in a manner that indicated the girl had no wish for further conversation. Perhaps it was better that way. Besides, Jenny knew that she had made her point.

Jenny stopped in the dining-room to order a breakfast tray for Mrs Ramsden. Then she went back to the bungalow. 'I'm going to help you wash and change into a fresh nightie,' she said soothingly, as she parted the curtains and opened the window. 'I don't think the doctor will be long.'

'Thank you, Jenny.' Mrs Ramsden stretched out a weak hand to her. 'I'm sorry to do this to you.'

'Nonsense. I enjoy being with you.' She took the hand and gave it a reassuring squeeze, and then began to make the older woman comfortable.

'You do this all so well,' Mrs Ramsden said a little later, when she was lying back against the freshly plumped-up pillows.

'I've had lots of practice.' Just then there was a knock at the door. 'That will be your breakfast.'

'Oh, my dear, I don't think I could eat a thing,' Mrs Ramsden protested weakly.

'Yes, you can.' Jenny went to the door and came back with the tray. 'Light but nourishing—just what you need.' With experience born of long months of nursing she persuaded Mrs Ramsden to have a spoonful of the soft-boiled egg, and then helped her with the remainder of her breakfast.

By the time the doctor came a little colour had returned to the older woman's cheeks. He took her temperature, listened to her chest, touched here and prodded there. At last, satisfied, he straightened. Going to the dressing-table, he looked over the array of pills that stood there.

'Will I be all right, doctor?' Mrs Ramsden asked anxiously.

'You will be fine in a day or two,' he said reassuringly. 'This is nothing serious, just a slight recurrence of the trouble you had before. I think the mountain air has done you a lot of good. And '—he smiled at Jenny—'you have a good nurse.'

As he took up his stethoscope and put the instruments back into his bag, he instructed Jenny on what to do. 'I'd like Mrs Ramsden to stay in bed today, and perhaps tomorrow,' he said. 'Then she can get up again, but she must have lots of rest. And of course, she must go on with her pills.' At the door he turned. 'How is the foot?'

'Much better.' Jenny smiled up at him.

'You're looking a little peaky yourself.' The doctor was regarding her searchingly. 'Don't you feel well?'

'There was a dance last night. I guess I went to bed a little late and missed out on some of my beauty sleep.'

'These youngsters.' He grinned across the room at Mrs Ramsden. 'Never can crowd enough hours into their days, can they? Now remember—lots of rest for a day or two, and if there should be any problems you know where to get hold of me.'

When Mrs Ramsden had had her medicine, Jenny found a magazine, pulled up a chair beside the bed and began to read to her. After a few minutes the older woman closed her eyes, and Jenny could tell by her rhythmic breathing that she was asleep.

Jenny put the magazine aside and went to the window. The morning mist had lifted from the mountains and the peaks were clear and bright in the sunshine. It was a lovely day, a day for walking and climbing, but Jenny had no regrets that she could not be out in the open. She was sorry that Mrs Ramsden was not well, but she was glad nevertheless of the excuse this gave her to stay in the bungalow.

Relations with Ann had never been good, and now there would be a strain with Andrew too. Perhaps if she did not see him for a day or two a surface friendliness might return. She hoped so, for they were thrown together so much in the narrowness of hotel life that a strain would be uncomfortable.

Her relationship with Ross was something different. The thought that she would not see him again— for it was clear that this would be so after last night—held so much pain that she tried to shut the thought from her mind.

And yet she was thankful now that she had not yet had a chance to tell Mrs Ramsden of her longing to go back to England. It was obvious that the older woman really did need care—not constant care, but someone to be around for the times when she was not well. So Jenny must stay. Eventually the holiday would come to an end, but until then there was nothing for it but to put on a brave face and an attitude of non-caring until that time came.

'Jenny . . .' She turned from the window and saw that Mrs Ramsden had awakened and was watching her. She went quickly to the bed.

'Yes?'

'The dance last night . . . You enjoyed it?'

'Very much.'

'Andrew was attentive?'

'Yes,' Jenny smiled, 'he was very nice.'

'I'm so glad. And Mr Sundy . . . was he there?'

'Ross . . .' Jenny paused, making a determined effort to keep her voice steady. Would it always be so difficult to speak his name? 'Yes, Ross was there too.'

'I heard the doctor say you looked peaky.' The older woman hesitated, and her eyes were troubled. 'Nothing—happened last night?'

'No.' Jenny smiled brightly. Mrs Ramsden was more shrewd than she had imagined. 'Everything was very nice. I'm just a little tired, I went to bed so late. Now, please, you mustn't worry about me. It's not good for you.'

The day passed uneventfully. By next morning Mrs Ramsden seemed much better, and on the third day Jenny knew she could take her back into the garden. Much as she had been glad of the excuse to stay in the bungalow, by now she had recovered much of her composure, and it was nice to be outside again. She sat with Mrs Ramsden, enjoying the touch of the sun on her face and arms, and the merry singing of the birds in the trees. She gazed into the mountains and at the forested slopes in the distance.

When Mrs Langley joined Mrs Ramsden in the garden Jenny walked down to the river. For some reason the rushing water seemed always to have a calming influence on her. By the time she returned to give Mrs Ramsden her medicine, she was happier than she had been since the evening of the dance.

It was two days later that letters arrived from Lynn. There was a thick one for her mother, with pictures of the baby, and a thinner one for Jenny. Jenny read the first part of the letter smiling with amusement and nostalgia. It contained mainly village gossip, gentle and yet at the same time pointed and funny, and once again a wave of home-sickness swept over her.

It was the second part of the letter that jolted her to attention. She read it once, very fast, and then read it again more slowly. Then she put the letter down on her lap and gazed thoughtfully into the mountains.

'The Stewarts really did see Neil Donaldson in your forests,' Lynn had written. 'Perhaps you thought the reason I mentioned him was so that you would agree to accompany Mother—but no, I'm quite sure of my facts. You see, Jenny, it was through the Stewarts that I heard of the hotel where you're staying. Please, Jenny, dear, don't let all this upset you. Mom had already mentioned that you couldn't find Neil, and I've been thinking—perhaps Neil left the Drakensberg shortly before your arrival, and the other forester—Mr Sundy—is new there, and never met him. Whatever the true facts, I really don't imagine there's any mystery about it at all.'

So Neil *had* lived in these parts. Much as Jenny had allowed herself to be persuaded otherwise, she thought now that somewhere at the back of her mind, she had always known it. She had allowed Ross to pull the wool over her eyes.

Just as she knew that Neil had been there, so she knew too that Ross had met him and had had dealings with him. She remembered only too well the wary look in his eyes whenever Neil's name had been mentioned.

At first she had wanted to penetrate the mystery, but as her love for Ross had grown, she had allowed herself to forget Neil, had allowed herself to believe Ross. Was this what love did to one?

And now—now that she knew for certain that Neil had in fact been here—what could she do? She could not leave the situation as it was. Her loyalty to Neil and the affection with which she remembered him were too great for that. If Neil was in trouble of some sort, which all the facts seemed to indicate, she wanted to know about it. She wanted to be able to help him. Just as he had always helped her when she was in trouble.

'Never mind, Jin-Jin,' was what he used to say. Jin-Jin—the pet name he had used whenever she was in disgrace or unhappy or nervous or frightened. Neil had been so much a part of her childhood. How could she have forgotten him just because she had fallen in love with Ross?

There remained the question—what was she to do? There was only one answer, of course. She must go to see Ross and confront him with the letter. She must refuse to accept his vagueness and demand to be told the truth. Ross would try to fob her off. Probably he would be angry. But she would have to insist.

Sadly she told herself that it would be easier now to accept his anger than it had been before, for she had nothing left to lose by provoking it. Jenny realised that what had been between them was something so fragile that now it was shattered, it was as if it had never existed at all—at least, that was how Ross would see it.

Much as she dreaded the thought of confronting Ross she knew it was something she must do. Now it was her loyalty to Neil which must come before anything else.

Tomorrow. She would go tomorrow. That would give her time to rehearse in her mind what she would say. She hoped, with little confidence, that between now and tomorrow she might gather enough strength to face Ross without breaking down.

Jenny slept very little that night. The words she intended using revolved ceaselessly in her mind. She was frightened, and at the same time sad, for she knew that once she had challenged Ross with her knowledge—and challenge was what it was—he would think she did not trust him, and might not want to see her again. Even this could not deter her, she told herself sternly.

She dressed carefully next morning—navy slacks

and a crisp floral shirt, open at the neck; hair brushed until it shone, and just enough make-up to bring out the golden sheen of her sun-kissed skin. And even as she chided herself for going to all this trouble, she knew, helplessly, that it was something she had to do.

'You're quite certain you'll be all right?' she asked Mrs Ramsden when she had settled her in the garden, a forlorn hope rising within her that the older woman might need her, and that the moment of crisis could be postponed for just a little while longer.

But no. 'I'll be fine,' Mrs Ramsden smiled at her. 'I'm so glad you have a chance to go out again. Go walking, my dear, and enjoy yourself.'

Enjoy! If Mrs Ramsden only knew what lay ahead of her.

# CHAPTER TEN

It was a lovely day. Wisps of cloud hung above the highest peaks, and the air was crisp and exhilarating, fragrant with the scent of wild flowers. Normally Jenny would have drunk in to the full the beauty all around her, but today her eyes travelled only from the path before her to the distant green of the forest. She was filled with a despairing bleakness. Was she being unutterably stupid to put her loyalty first, and so cast aside the last chance of happiness with the man she loved?

She came at last to the jungle, and from there to the forest. With a pounding heart she walked the last stretch to the cottage in the clearing. It looked deserted. If Ross had been here his dog would already be bounding up to her. She knocked at the door, but as she had anticipated, there was no reply. Well, she would wait. It would be too easy just to walk back again, Ross often came back to the cottage at about this time. Nothing would be lost in waiting, and if he did not come she would just have to try again another day.

It came to her all at once how tired she was.

Her foot was so much better now, but she still tired easily, and it had been a long walk. Also, she had slept only fitfully the night before. More than anything else, she had a craving for a cup of tea.

Hesitantly she pushed open the door of the cottage and went inside. As before, the room she was in was scrupulously neat and very clean, and once again it occurred to her that Ross was a very self-sufficient man. In the nook which served as a kitchenette she saw that the kettle was filled with clean water. After hunting a few moments she found a packet of matches and lit the gas-ring.

While she waited for the kettle to boil she strolled over to the bookcase and looked at Ross's books. Taking out one or two, Jenny saw that they had been read often and, she guessed, with enjoyment. She saw many of her own favourites, but there were also books on forestry, on birds and on the habits of wild animals. There was even a book on bush-men paintings. She began to page through it, and the replicas of the rock-paintings brought back in all its vividness the last wonderful day she had spent with Ross. Her eyes were blurred as she put the book back on its shelf.

When she heard the hissing of the kettle she went over to the gas-ring. She found a cup and saucer, but could not find the tea. She opened a small cup-board which contained groceries, but did not see it. Where did Ross keep it? Frowning, she glanced around. Her eyes alighted on a little chest of drawers. On it were a pipe, a book and a torch. Could he possibly keep the tea here? It was unlikely, of course, but perhaps he had put it down unintentionally while he was busy with his pipe. Hardly thinking that she was invading another person's privacy, she moved the notebook and the torch. She saw the tea was not there. And then she heard something fall. With a metallic clink the thing fell to the ground behind the chest of drawers. It must be something that Ross would miss. She must find it and put it back.

She dropped to her knees and bent her head beneath the chest of drawers. Screwing up her eyes, she searched in the darkness beneath the chest of drawers, but she could see nothing. Then she reached forward, gently moving her hand over the ground beneath the chest. At first she felt only the floor, then her hand touched something hard and cold—something metal. She closed her fingers around the object and got to her feet.

She looked at the thing she had picked up and found herself trembling so that she had to put out a hand to the chest of drawers to support herself. It could not be—but it was! A medallion with a picture of a bear upon it. The medallion was smooth around the edges, as if it had been held many times between a person's fingers. The picture was almost obscured, but there remained enough of it for her to recognise it.

With a beating heart she turned the medallion over, and there, as she knew it would be, was the scratched letter 'N'. Neil's medallion. Until now, until the moment she had held it in her hands, she had forgotten its existence. He had always carried it with him, no matter where he went. It had always held a special significance for him. Standing there in Ross's cottage, with her eyes closed and the medallion in her hand, Jenny could hear Neil saying, 'I'll always keep this, Jin-Jin. It brings me luck.'

Still trembling, she went back to the gas-ring. More than ever now she needed something warm to drink. Again she opened the little grocery cupboard, and there, half hidden behind a packet of biscuits, she saw the packet of tea. How silly of her to have overlooked it the first time.

And yet—perhaps she had been meant to overlook the tea. Perhaps something stronger than herself had induced her to look around the room so that she would find the medallion.

She slipped the medallion into the pocket of her slacks. Then she took a tea-bag, placed it in the cup, took the kettle from the gas-ring and poured the boiling water into the cup. She found an open packet of biscuits, and went to sit at the table. Slowly she began to sip the tea. The warmth of the scalding liquid steadied her, until even the trembling of her hands began to still.

What did the medallion mean? Neil had been here—he had actually been in this cottage. That much was obvious. Had he lived here? That would account for the medallion which had somehow slipped behind the chest of drawers. But why was Ross so adamant that he did not know Neil? And where was Neil now?

So absorbed was she in her thoughts that she

did not hear the sounds outside the cottage. She gave a startled exclamation when the door was flung open and a pile of fur hurled itself against her. A wet nose nuzzled against her, and there was a series of delighted little squeals and barks.

'Migs!' Jenny put her arm around the excited dog and looked over its head into the eyes of the man who had entered the cottage.

'Ross!' She could feel that the colour had drained from her cheeks. She tried to get to her feet.

'Jenny!' The eyes that had been puzzled and wary at the knowledge that someone was in his cottage had filled with such warmth that she felt weak at the knees. 'Jenny!' With one swift step he was across the room, had pulled the excited dog away from her, and was drawing Jenny to her feet.

'Ross, you don't mind . . . ?' Her voice was jerky with nerves.

'Mind!'

'You weren't here, and . . . and I was so tired and thirsty, so . . . so I made myself some tea.' The colour that had left her cheeks had surged back into them, and she was flushing beneath his gaze. For a moment she could not think about Neil. The happiness she felt at Ross's nearness was too overpowering.

'My dear girl, I'm delighted! Let me look at you.' He held her away from him, the colour in his eyes deepening. Then he pulled her close to him. 'Don't you know that I take it as a compliment that you made yourself at home here?'

'You do?'

'Yes,' he said quietly. 'Because that's what it should be to you.'

'Oh!' She looked up at him, a little stunned, hardly trusting herself to interpret his words in the way she wanted so much to do.

'I thought after the other night . . . Oh, but that's over now.' Suddenly his lips were on hers, and she was kissing him back, her body aflame with treacherous sensations. At last he stopped and led her back to her chair. 'I'm so glad you made the first start,' he said. 'That *is* why you came, Jenny, isn't it? I was so jealous when I saw Andrew kissing you that I . . .'

'He kissed me to make you jealous,' she said.

'Did he?' Ross smiled suddenly. 'Fancy that! Oh, Jenny, bless you for coming back!'

'I . . .' The feelings he produced in her were so overpowering that she was tempted to say nothing of the reason for her coming, to disregard the medallion that burnt like a flame in her pocket. But she knew with sudden clarity that much as she wanted him, much as she wanted only to feel his arms close about her once more, she could not live with this terrible doubt and suspicion. She knew that there could be no secrecy between her and the man she loved.

'Ross . . .' She pulled away from him. She could not bear to be so near to him if she was going to speak firmly and dispassionately. 'Ross, I came because of a letter.'

'A letter?' The sparkle had left his eyes, and he was looking puzzled.

'A letter from Mrs Ramsden's daughter.'

'Oh!'

'There was something in it . . . Ross, I have to ask you something.'

'All right, Jenny.' He moved away from her, took the pipe from his chest of drawers and began to light it. 'I just hope this won't be something we'll both regret—but ask.'

'Ross, Lynn is certain Neil Donaldson was seen here.'

'Jenny . . .' he began.

'I'm sorry, Ross, I know you don't like to talk about him, but I must. Neil met some people called Stewart—I told you that once before. He talked to them. The Stewarts told Lynn about their meeting.'

'The Drakensberg are a very long range of mountains,' Ross observed quietly.

'That's what I had begun to think too. But Lynn . . . Lynn said the Stewarts told her the name of the hotel they stayed at. It's our hotel. That was how Lynn got to know about it in the first place.'

It was very quiet in the room. Only the sound of Migs' panting broke the stillness. Ross was very busy with his pipe. At last he said, 'These people— Stewart, did you say was their name?—they must have made a mistake.'

'No.'

'There is no Neil Donaldson here.'

'Isn't it possible that Neil lived here before you did?' She was still trying to provide him with a way out.

'No, Jenny, I don't think it is.' He was speaking very quietly. 'I would have known.'

So he did not want to admit it. There was an anguish within her as she put her hand into her pocket and drew out the worn piece of metal. 'Ross,' she said, her eyes watching his face, 'then what is this?'

At the sight of the medallion he looked visibly shaken. For a moment she thought he did not breathe. Only a moment, then he had regained his composure once more.

'What about it?' he asked, giving it only a cursory glance. 'What is that—a child's toy or something?'

'This belongs to Neil.'

'How do you know?' There was a bitterness in his face that wrenched at her heart. 'You haven't seen Neil for years. And a thing like that—it's not unique. There must be hundreds of similar ones.'

'Similar—yes. But not quite like this.' She held it out to him. 'You see, it has an " N " scratched on to it. Ross . . . Ross, I know it's Neil's. It's an inexpensive little thing, but it meant a lot to him. He carried it with him always.'

'Where did you find it?' he asked.

'Behind your chest of drawers.'

'What!' he said incredulously.

'I think . . . I think it may have been on the skirting behind the chest of drawers, and then it dropped . . . I found it on the floor.'

'So,' he said in a tone she had never heard him use before. 'You came to my cottage to pry.'

'No. No, Ross!'

'You waited until I was out,' he went on relentlessly, 'then you came and started going through my things.'

'Oh, no. It wasn't like that. I couldn't find the tea . . . You see . . .'

'Well?' He looked very deliberately at her cup.

'I looked in the grocery cupboard, and couldn't find it.' She was speaking too quickly, the words tumbling over one another in her nervousness. 'Oh, it was there, but I only saw it afterwards. I went up to the chest of drawers, and then . . . I must have moved something. I heard something fall . . . I bent down to see what it was . . . and I found the medallion.'

'You must have thought me a fool when I came in and was so happy to find you.' His eyes had never looked so disdainful.

'Oh, no!'

'Yes. I so very nearly said even more than I did. You'd have thought me even more foolish.' He took a slow deliberate puff. 'And all the time you didn't come for me at all. You only came because of Neil Donaldson.'

'But, Ross, I had to find him, don't you see?'

'But I'd already told you he wasn't there. Don't you believe me, Jenny? Don't you trust me?'

*I love you. I trust you. I'd trust you with my life. But in this one thing I don't know what to believe.*

'I trust you,' she said miserably.

'You have a strange way of showing it. What is this obsession about Neil Donaldson?' He had come

156

close to her, and his hands gripped her arms tightly, hurting her. 'What does he mean to you?'

'He's a boy I was fond of,' she said desperately. 'I know he's here somewhere, and I want to find him. Ross, let go of my arms! You're hurting me.'

'Not as much as I would like to.' He dropped her arms and bit savagely at his pipe. 'At last I understand now, Jenny. You're in love with a boy you haven't laid eyes on for years.'

'It's not that,' she protested.

'Yes! You've convinced yourself of something. Of utter nonsense. Why can't you fall in love with a proper man instead of a . . . a phantom?'

I love *you*, she wanted to shout. But she only said, 'You're twisting things, Ross.'

'Am I?'

'All I ask is that you tell me about the medallion.'

'I don't know how it got here,' he said flatly. 'What's more, I couldn't care less.' He had her arm again, and was propelling her out of his cottage. 'I want you to go now. Don't come back, ever. You'll find nothing here, Jenny.'

'Ross . . .' she pleaded.

'The cottage will be locked from now on.'

'You make it sound as if I'm a thief,' she said, choking back the tears. 'I didn't think you'd mind me coming here, making tea because I was thirsty . . .'

'If that's all you'd come for I'd have been the happiest man on earth—you saw my reaction. But you came to pry. You slunk in here when I was away —to try to find out something about this man you're

157

so obsessed with. That's something I cannot tolerate.'

'Ross . . .' she began, wondering what she could say to appease him, but he stood in the doorway, white through his tan, as immovable as a piece of granite.

'Please go, Jenny.'

'All right.' She pushed past him. The tears were beginning to fall. He made no move to comfort her, or to check her leaving. She was stumbling through the clearing when the dog hurled itself out of the cottage. Sensing her distress, it nuzzled against her, nibbling at her hand. Bending down, Jenny buried her face in the warm coat, but then she heard Ross calling. Migs stopped licking her. The dog's head was turned towards the cottage. 'Migs!' Again the command rang out, and reluctantly the animal moved away from her and back to its master.

It seemed a long way back to the hotel. Jenny's feet dragged through the forest and through the jungle. Once she stumbled over a tangle of roots and tore her hand on the rough bark of a tree. Somehow the sight of the graze seemed so in keeping with her general mood of despair that she did not even stop when she reached the stream.

It was all over. Neil—Neil was somewhere here, or had been, and it seemed unlikely now that she would find him.

And Ross. Ross thought of her as a spy, as an immature girl, obsessed and neurotic. His parting words rang in her ears: 'Don't come here again.' No impulsive words these, for she knew that he meant them. Knew too that wild horses would not drag her back to the cottage in the clearing.

All she could hope for now was that she could spend the rest of the time in the Drakensberg without running into him again.

# CHAPTER ELEVEN

Soon after her return from the forest Jenny had written to the Forestry Department, asking for information about Neil Donaldson. So far, a month later, there had been no reply, and Jenny was beginning to grow anxious. In just over a week they would be returning to England, and she felt that if she did not find Neil before then she would never find him.

It had become very important to her that she should find him. She had ruined things with Ross. Jenny had never been back to the forest since that terrible day, nor had Ross made any move towards her. The friendly relationship with Andrew had ended too. She was lonely now in the evenings, for since the night of the dance Andrew had begun to spend more and more time with Ann.

At least as far as Neil was concerned she did not want things to be spoiled. It was not enough that Ross should tell her he did not know him. The two men must have had a private feud or argument that she knew nothing about. But if Neil was in these parts she wanted to know it, wanted to see him, to have a chat to him before going back to England and making a new life for herself.

The old life was over, but it had been important to her. Neil had been a part of that life. If she could just see him once more, it would be like laying a ghost. She felt that she could then start anew with nothing to hold her back—nothing except her longing for Ross, and that was something she would have to learn to live with.

Jenny had been giving much thought to her future of late, and there were several fields that she was considering. Sometimes she thought she would become a teacher, and at other times it was the idea of nursing that appealed to her. But it was obvious that she had no vocation for either of these careers, she thought ruefully, for then there would be no decision to make. As it was, she must come to a decision soon. That she might get married was an eventuality she hardly considered. There was only one man in the world for her, and Ross had made it clear what he thought of her.

She had been sitting in front of the open brick fireplace in the lounge. Although it was mid-morning it was so cold that a fire had been lit. Moodily Jenny got to her feet and crossed to the window and looked out. Still raining. It had been raining for three days now, a pouring, chilling rain that swirled and eddied about the trees, turning the garden and the sandy paths into muddy quagmires.

If only the rain would end! Longingly she thought of the many days of brilliant sunshine she had spent out of doors. Soon they would be going back to

England and more rain. She had looked forward to spending her last days in the Drakensberg acquiring a tan that would stay with her for a while, but the dismal scene that met her eyes made that hope seem forlorn. She turned from the window and made her way back to the fire.

'Jenny.' Mrs Ramsden came into the lounge just then, and held out a letter to her. 'Post for you.'

'Thank you.' She took the envelope, her brow wrinkling at sight of the South African stamp. Who could be writing to her? For a wild moment she thought of Ross, and with trembling hands she tore open the envelope. Then she saw the official letter-head. It was from the Forestry Department.

Stifling her momentary disappointment, she began to read—only to be confronted by even more disappointment. Neil Donaldson was not known to them. To their knowledge there was no forester of that name. If they could be of any further assistance to her she could correspond with them again.

'Bad news?' She looked up to find Mrs Ramsden watching her.

'I'm afraid so,' Jenny said dully.

'It's not . . .'—the woman hesitated, 'it's not from Mr Sundy?'

'Oh, no.' Jenny found herself colouring. So Mrs Ramsden had wondered whether she would be hearing from Ross. 'I wasn't expecting a letter from Ross. No—it's from the Forestry Department. They've never heard of Neil.'

'Oh, Jenny, I'm sorry.' Mrs Ramsden's kind brown eyes had filled with concern. 'So there really must have been a mistake.'

'It seems like it.'

'My dear,' the older woman stretched out a hand to the girl, 'I know you're disappointed, and yet . . . I don't know why, but I still think you'll find him one day. Not here, of course, but somewhere.'

'I don't think so. Not now.' Jenny was about to say more, then as she thought better of it, she stopped. She could not tell Mrs Ramsden that her main thought at this moment was not Neil but of Ross. Neil . . . Neil had been away from her for a long time. Some day, perhaps, as Mrs Ramsden had said, they might meet again, though now, after reading this letter, she did not think so.

It was her desire to find Neil that had destroyed the relationship with the man she loved. An obsession, Ross had called it. Could it be that Ross really had been speaking the truth when he had disclaimed any knowledge of Neil? But no—even now, she could not convince herself that his wariness at any mention of Neil had been just a product of her imagination. Just as the medallion had not been imagined. That had belonged to Neil—there could be no doubt about that. Jenny thought of the Stewarts, who had been so certain that this was where they had seen him. She believed that they had in fact met him. But they were wrong in thinking Neil was a forester. In the same way all Jenny's thoughts and deductions obviously had been wrong.

Possibilities crowded her mind. Neil had always loved the outdoor life. Perhaps he had come to these mountains on a climbing holiday, and while he was here he had met up with the Stewarts. Perhaps for some reason he had had occasion to visit Ross's cottage in the forest, and had dropped the medallion. Then again, it could have dropped from his pocket, been picked up by the dog, or even by Ross himself, and been brought into the cottage. Ross would have been unaware to whom it belonged. Even if he had seen it, he would have attached no importance to it, for it looked like nothing more than the child's treasure it was meant to be. It would have significance for nobody but Neil.

Of these two possibilities she was inclined to favour the former, for that would explain Ross's attitude. Could it be that Ross had come across Neil in the forests, become friendly with him, and then caught him out in some type of bad behaviour? It did not seem likely, for this would not be in character with the boy she remembered, but perhaps she was behaving like a mother who can believe nothing ill of her child. After all, it was so many years since she had last seen Neil. If something *had* happened between the two men, something that had angered or antagonised Ross, this might account for his reluctance to talk about Neil. It would also account for his bitterness when she persisted in her efforts to find him. She knew now that he had been speaking the truth when he had said Neil was not a forester.

'Sorry to be going back home soon?' Mrs Ramsden's words broke into her thoughts.

'A little.' She smiled at the older woman. 'Though I shouldn't be. It's time I got my life organised.'

'But you have enjoyed it here?'

'So much.'

'I just thought . . . the last few days . . . perhaps you were beginning to get a little bored,' Mrs Ramsden said hesitantly.

'Oh, no.' Jenny was remorseful. 'Perhaps it's the rain that's been making me grouchy. These mountains —they're so beautiful. I don't think I could ever get tired of them.'

'Perhaps the sun will shine again soon,' said Mrs Ramsden hopefully.

'Oh, I hope so! I want to get out . . . to walk.' And to speak to Ross. Just once more. Just to know that when she left these mountains it would be with the knowledge that there was no bitterness between them. She wanted Ross to know that she did not distrust him. She did not allow herself to hope for more than that.

It rained again the next day, and the next, but on the third day Jenny woke to see the sun filtering through the curtains, and when she slid out of bed and ran to the window she could see the mountains for the first time in days. Only the highest peaks were obliterated by cloud. But the mist would lift from the peaks, for the rain had stopped.

Jenny dressed quickly and went into the garden. The flower beds were muddy, and small pools of water still lay in depressions in the paths, but already the sun was beginning to dry the grass, and the sandy drive that led up to the hotel looked as if it would soon be negotiable once more. Along with the special smell that seemed to linger when the rain had ended, there was an air of freshness and newness

165

that was intoxicating.

By the time Jenny met Mrs Ramsden for breakfast she was ravenous. ' I can see you've been making the most of the morning.' The older woman smiled, looking at the glowing cheeks and shining eyes. ' We'll be able to enjoy the sun today.'

' I want to go out walking after breakfast,' Jenny told her.

' Do you think it's wise?'

' Oh, yes, I'm sure the rain is over.' Jenny glanced through the dining-room window at the cloudless blue sky. ' I think I'll go as soon as I've settled you in the garden.'

Now that the weather had cleared Jenny was gripped with a strange impatience. Time was running out. Mountain weather could be unpredictable. There could quite easily be another rainy spell. And she wanted to see Ross just once before they left for England.

' I'll be all right,' she smiled at Mrs Ramsden. ' I know how to take care of myself.'

After breakfast Jenny settled Mrs Ramsden in her usual seat in the garden. She was already on the path that led to the forest when, on an impulse, she returned to the hotel, went back to the bungalow, looked in the mirror, and then opened the wardrobe. She hesitated a few moments before taking out the shirt and trousers she had worn on that second, wonderful outing with Ross. She had brushed her hair earlier that morning, but now she brushed it again, till it hung loose and swinging about her face. Then she started out again.

It was a lovely day, and though Jenny was tense with conflicting emotions, she could not help enjoying being out of doors again. For days the mountains had been hidden by a shroud of cloud and rain. Now even the highest peaks were clear as the morning mist lifted. The veld, often brown and a little drab, was flushed with a delicate green and studded with wild flowers that danced and swayed in the breeze. Even the smell was different. She had noticed it in the hotel garden earlier that morning, but here in the veld, it was even more apparent. The rain had settled the dust of the bush, and the air was pervaded with the lovely odour of growing things.

Jenny stopped when she came to the water. She had become accustomed to crossing streams and thought nothing of taking off her shoes and stepping from boulder to boulder, even wading through the water whenever it was necessary. But the rain had turned the stream into a fast-flowing river, a rushing torrent which overflowed on to either side of its banks and was several inches higher than the rocks.

She surveyed the scene in dismay. The water looked so very fast and strong. Could she make it? Her dismay was compounded of nervousness and vanity. If she crossed this river she would have to roll up her slacks as far as they would go, and they would get creased, perhaps wet. She would look bedraggled when Ross saw her—and she had so much wanted to look her best.

But there was no alternative. After rolling her slacks to her knees, Jenny began, very cautiously, to cross the river. The water was even faster and deeper than she had imagined. There was a bad moment when she stood on a slippery boulder and thought she would fall. She flung out her arms and managed to save herself, but not without soaking her clothes. At last she reached the other side. She breathed deeply as she rolled down her slacks once more. They were wet and creased, and she wondered ruefully whether they would have dried by the time she saw Ross.

Presently Jenny came to the jungle. She entered that dim silent world, and the smell hit her with a shock. There was a rank odour of damp and mouldering vegetation that was sickening. She realised that here the sun, which at best could penetrate only weakly through the tangled mass of vegetation, would take much longer to effect the drying process that was already going on elsewhere.

The path through the jungle was slippery and very muddy, and there were patches where Jenny found the going really difficult. Before long the soles of her shoes became so clogged with mud that each step was a struggle. Here and there she came to quagmires which were impassable, and which she had to skirt by walking over the tangles of roots and moss. Even this was more difficult than she had expected, and it was not long before her slacks were covered with mud and burrs and a peculiar weed with short sharp thorn-like needles which clung tenaciously to her clothes.

As the going became more and more difficult, so her discouragement grew. Mrs Ramsden had been right when she had advised her to wait a few days. There was still some way to go. Should she turn back? She was about to retrace her steps when she remembered how little time she had left. Soon they would be going back to England. It could rain again. Or Mrs Ramsden could have a relapse of her illness, and then Jenny would be unable to leave her. If that happened there might not be another chance to see Ross.

There was nothing for it. She had got this far and she would go on. Once, briefly, the thought came to her that she might be doing all this in vain. Ross might not be at the cottage when she got there. But she had had the foresight to bring with her a pencil and paper. Even if Ross was not there, she could leave a note, explain as much as it was possible to put on to paper, and hope that he would come to see her to say goodbye.

She was almost through the jungle when she came around a bend and stopped, her heart sinking. Before her in the path lay a patch of mud which was worse than all the others she had encountered. It was a horrible slithery-looking quagmire, and Jenny knew at once that it would be impossible to walk through the squishy mess. If she stepped into it she would be bogged down completely. She looked to each side of it. The alternatives were not much more attractive. On the right side of the path loomed the jungle at its thickest and most impenetrable. On the left, admittedly, there were gaps between the trees, but she could see that she would get scratched and torn in the tangled mass of hanging roots and twisting thorny branches.

She could not stay where she was, so she chose the left side, bent to part the undergrowth, and took a step into it. Her foot sank in a soft mass of vegetable matter and she shuddered. After a moment she followed resolutely with the other foot, then pushed her way further. Each step was a mammoth undertaking. She pushed and pulled at roots and matted bark, and crawled beneath lichens and ferns while hanging branches tickled her neck and tore at her bare arms.

Once she stood on something smooth and coiled and elastic, and froze. There came into her mind a picture of the mamba which had slept behind the rock in the forest. For a moment she was transfixed with fear, not daring to look down, not knowing where to put her other foot. At last she forced herself to turn her eyes downwards to see what she was standing on. It was not a snake but a coiled spongy mass of roots. She breathed a sigh of relief, and went slowly on.

Inch by inch she worked her way through the jungle. The stretch of mud in the path before her had seemed no more than a matter of yards, but a few yards in the tangled undergrowth was like something she had read about in adventure stories about the Amazon.

She stopped once to rest, and looked down at the slacks and shirt that had been so smart and spruce that morning. By the time she got out of the jungle her clothes would not even be fit for a rag-bag. What a fool she had been to venture into the jungle when everything was still wet! In a day or two, when the sun had dried the path, she would have been able to make her way through with ease.

At least she would not return the way she had come—she had made up her mind about that. If Ross was not at the cottage she would wait until he arrived. He would have to take her back to the hotel by car, using the motor road on the far side of the forest.

Jenny was nearly back at the path when it happened. She had gripped a curtain of fern fronds, pulled them to one side, and pushed a foot through the gap. Finding that she could not quite reach the ground on the other side, she supported one foot on a tree trunk, pulled herself up, then jumped through to the other side. For a moment she thought she was plunging into nothingness, then her foot hit the ground. She reached out to grasp the branch of a tree, but the decaying matter came away in her hands. She slipped and fell.

For a moment she was winded. Then she tried to get to her feet—and could not. In falling she had turned her foot. It was the foot that had been hurt before and which had only recently healed. With a tremendous effort of will she tried to force herself to stand, but the pain was so intense that she moaned and fell back.

She could not stand, could not walk. She could not even hop, for she had nothing with which to support herself. With a shudder she sank back against the rotting mass. She tried to move her foot so that it would be comfortable—anything to ease the throbbing pain that was almost unbearable. She tried to console herself with the thought that perhaps in a little while she would feel better, then she might be able to get to her feet again. She could not just lie there.

Now that she was in one position, without moving, the cold of the jungle hit her. She felt the cold and the damp begin to seep through her body. Her bones ached. She began to wonder what the jungle was like at night.

Night! At the thought she had an uncontrollable fit of trembling. Lying here in the daytime was bad enough, but night in the jungle was something not to be thought of. And yet, much as she tried not to think about it, images, each more gruesome than the next, crowded her mind. Night would come early in the dim world of the jungle, and she could not be here when it did. Somehow she must be rescued before then.

She tried to turn her mind to other things. She thought of England, but the village and the cottage seemed unreal, as if they had existed a long time ago and in another world. Her mind turned to Mrs Ramsden. How worried she would be when Jenny did not return. There was something reassuring in that thought. Of course, Mrs Ramsden would not worry immediately. When Jenny was not at the hotel for lunch her friend would probably think she had taken advantage of the lovely weather and decided to make a day of it. It would be in the evening, when darkness fell and still Jenny was not back, that Mrs Ramsden would begin to worry in earnest. She would

172

talk to Andrew, and they would discuss ways of finding her.

Would they think of looking for her in the jungle? Jenny had not taken the precaution of saying where she was going. Even if they thought of trying this route, they would find it impossible to walk through the undergrowth in the dark. Next morning, at the latest, they would come this way. Search parties would go out in different directions. At least one group of people must come this way. She would hear them coming and would shout to them, and they would find her. But before the morning came a night in the jungle . . .

Ross . . . Ross might not be far away. She had been almost through the jungle when she had slipped. But Ross did not know what had happened. There was no reason why he should look for her.

It grew colder, and the pain in her foot became worse. Jenny's eyes began to close. Crazy images began to surge through her mind. Once she opened her eyes, and jerked herself back to her surroundings. She wondered if she was delirious. Perhaps this was all just a bad dream from which she would waken with a shock of relief.

It grew colder still, but after a while Jenny did not mind so much any more. In her half dreaming, half waking state her discomfort mattered less and less. She no longer knew what was real and what was imagined. There was Andrew. He was smiling at her over the Scrabble board. And there was Ross. He was carrying her up the rocks to see the rock paintings. And there was a dog—Ross's dog? The dog was nibbling her hand, nuzzling against her, trying to move her with the pushing movements of its head and its paws.

And then the image of the dog superseded all the others, and the feel of the nibbling became irritating, and she opened her eyes and moved her hand to push the dog away. The dog stood beside her, making little mewing barks, trying to nudge her to her feet.

The dog was real! It had found her! Jenny was conscious now. Painfully she managed to wrench a shoe from her feet, and thrust it between the dog's jaws. 'Take it to him,' she gasped. 'Fetch him. Fetch him! Bring him here.'

The dog must have understood, for after a moment it ceased its frantic movements. For a long moment it stood beside Jenny, panting heavily. Then it bounded away through the tangled creepers.

It was so cold, and the pain was a numb throbbing that had become a part of her. Come, Ross. Come. I don't know how much longer I can stand it here. Please, Ross. Please come!

And then, mercifully, the cold and the pain began to dissolve, and she was no longer aware of her surroundings. At one stage she was vaguely aware of something pushing her, pulling her. Strong arms held her. There were barks and yaps and soothing words. And then even these images dissolved.

# CHAPTER TWELVE

Jenny was lying in a bed. She felt drowsy and content, and was filled with a lovely sense of lethargy. Her head did not hurt any more, but it felt heavy, and she could not open her eyes. Vaguely she remembered slipping, hurting her foot, lying in the cold and damp. Now she was warm, and so comfortable. A blanket had been placed gently about her, and something seemed to be wrapped around her feet.

She became aware that there was a person in the room with her. She tried to open her eyes, but it was too much of an effort, so she just went on lying quite still. There was movement in the room. She heard quiet footsteps, and a drawer closed, then someone stopped beside her and put a gentle hand to her cheek. A kiss, light as a butterfly, touched her forehead. Mother? No, it could not be Mother. Was it that nice lady, Mrs Ramsden?

Her head cleared a little more. Blurred images were beginning to float before her eyes. Remember . . . remember . . . What had happened . . . ? She tried to move her leg and felt a stab of pain. She lay quite still, then tried again. Once more the stab of pain.

The person beside her moved. 'Jenny . . .' It was a man's voice, soft and full of concern. 'Jin-Jin. Jin-Jin . . . Can you hear me? Oh, Jenny, Jenny darling, open your eyes. Tell me you're all right. Please, Jenny.' He was silent a while, then, when she did not respond: 'Jin-Jin! Jin-Jin, can you hear me?'

Memory flooding her. So many memories. Jin-Jin . . . Only one person called her Jin-Jin—Neil. Neil, for whom she had been looking. Neil had found her.

Confused. Everything was so confused. She had been looking for Neil, but Neil was not here. The dog. There had been a dog . . . She had told the dog to find Ross. Ross whom she loved. But Neil had found her. Neil was with her now.

'Jenny . . . Jenny, my darling, can you hear me? Please, Jenny. Jin-Jin, open your eyes.'

Open her eyes. She must open her eyes. The voice had been so full of love. For him—she must do it for him. For Neil. She could not see his face behind her closed lids, the face of the boy who had been her childhood. With a tremendous effort her eyes opened . . . slowly . . . slowly. The light in the room blurred the face that hung over her. And then the blurring cleared, and the remembered face of the boy who was Neil dissolved into the beloved face of the man who was Ross.

'Ross . . .'

'Jenny!' He was bending over her, his eyes warm and concerned. 'Jenny, you're all right?'

176

'Yes.' She moved her leg and then winced with pain. 'Oh, Ross, I'm so sore. I hurt all over . . .'

'No wonder! Presently, when you're a little stronger, you'll tell me all about it.'

'Yes. Ross, it was Migs . . . Migs found me.'

'Thank God for Migs,' he said soberly. 'Migs came to the cottage and pawed at the door. She raised a terrible row, so I came outside. I was about to get angry, and then—I saw your shoe in her mouth.'

'The shoe . . . I gave her my shoe . . .'

'You were unconscious when I found you.' He paused, searching her face. 'Thank goodness for that, because you'd have suffered even more if you'd been awake. Jenny . . . Jenny, what were you doing there in the jungle?'

'I came to see you. I couldn't walk along the path. The mud . . .'

'You should have waited till the path was dry.'

'I had to come. I had to tell you . . .'

'Tell me what?' His eyes were curiously alert now.

'That I'd been wrong about . . . about Neil.'

'I see.'

'And then, just now . . . I thought . . .' She fell silent. A fire burnt in the hearth, casting long shadows over the room, and she searched Ross's face, the craggy lines and the crevices thrown into relief by the flickering light. 'I couldn't have been dreaming. Ross, you are Neil, aren't you?'

He did not answer, but turned away from her abruptly, and she thought she saw his jaw stiffen.

177

He took his pipe from his pocket, and began to fill the bowl with tobacco. At last the stem of the pipe was between his lips and he took a puff. When he turned back to her his muscles had relaxed. 'Yes, Jenny,' he said, sitting down beside her bed and taking her hand in his. 'I'm Neil.'

'Oh, Ross!' The name came out quite naturally, and she knew it was the one she would always use. 'Ross, why?'

'It's a long story.' He was smiling now, and searching his eyes she realised that they at least were the eyes she remembered. Strange that she had never seen it before. Perhaps it was just that everything else about him had changed so much.

'I know you're full of questions, Jenny,' he said, 'and now, at last, I feel I can answer them.'

'You'll tell me why you pretended that . . . ?'

'Everything,' he interrupted her gently. 'But first I want to get some warm food into you.'

'I'm not hungry,' she protested quickly, feeling she could wait no longer to hear what he had to say.

'Of course you are. You're always hungry— remember?' He stopped smiling and said more seriously, 'You were in the jungle a long time, Jenny. You were cold and wet when I brought you here, and you've had nothing to eat since breakfast. You must be starving.'

'What time is it?' she asked as he brought a bowl of broth over to her bed, and began to feed her.

'After eight,' he said briefly.

'But then it must be dark! Mrs Ramsden!' Her hand flew to her mouth. 'I must get back to the hotel.'

'Impossible,' he said cheerfully, spooning the soup gently between her lips. 'Not till tomorrow, and then only if the roads are dry.'

'You mean—I'm to spend the night here with you?' she asked uncertainly.

'That's right.' He laughed at her expression on her face. 'Completely unchaperoned.'

'Oh . . .' She should not feel the way she did about it, especially now that she knew he was Neil. And yet he was not Neil. He was not the boy she remembered. He was Ross. Ross, who by a look or a touch could set her pulses beating and the blood racing in her veins.

'Since you've taken my bed I'll be sleeping there.' She followed the line of his finger and saw that he had made himself a makeshift bed by the fire.

'But . . . Ross, Mrs Ramsden will be worried. She'll have search parties out after me.'

'Everything's been taken care of. You see, Jenny, I don't have my car here. The road through the forest is strictly a dry-weather one, impassable after the rains we've been having. My car is at the bottom of the mountain.'

'Oh!'

'And if you're considering the wheelbarrow—let me remind you of the quagmires you walked through.'

'I've been an idiot, haven't I?' she said remorsefully. 'Mrs Ramsden told me to wait till things dried up. Ross, does she really know where I am?'

'Really,' he assured her. 'After I got you into bed and made you comfortable, I sent down a message with one of the woodcutters who lives in a little house not far from here. He came back an hour ago with a note.'

' Then she's not worried?'

' I don't suppose she's happy about the situation, but she's not worried.'

' I'm glad.' They were silent for a while. There was something inexplicably cosy about the atmosphere in the cottage—the leaping firelight, the neat clean room. Ross sitting beside her bed, spooning the warm soup into her mouth. Migs squatting at his feet, watching them both with undisguised delight.

She ought to be happy—happier than she now was. All these weeks she had been searching for Neil, and now at last she had found him. But it was Neil of her childhood for whom she had been searching. It was Ross, a mature man, she had found—and fallen in love with. And though she was happy they could be together, however briefly, she knew with every fibre of her being that she wanted more than this. Ross was fond of her—not at all strange now that she knew who he was—but she guessed that affection to be no more than the feeling of a very good friend. And she . . . she wanted so very much more.

' You were going to tell me why you came to see me,' he said at last.

' Oh, no,' said Jenny. ' You have a lot of explaining to do.'

' I know that. But I want you to talk first.'

She wanted to resist him, but there was a gentle authority in his voice before which she had to yield. ' I wanted to see you, speak to you. We're going back to England in a few days, and I couldn't go without telling you I'd been wrong.'

'Wrong about what?'

'About . . .' She paused. 'But, Ross, it sounds so silly now.'

'I don't think so.'

'But now . . . now that I know who you are . . .' she went on.

'If it will make things easier, don't think of me as Neil. Just for the telling.'

'Well,' she said trying to organise her thoughts, 'you kept saying there was no Neil Donaldson—that there was no forester by that name. After a while I began to think that must be true, but then—then I found the medallion.'

'My precious bear!' He laughed softly. 'What a shock it was when you produced it.'

'Couldn't you have told me then?'

'No. I wasn't ready for it. You'll understand everything when I explain, Jenny.'

'But you were so angry.'

'Partly to cover up for my shock. But also I was so happy to see you, and then I thought you'd just come to pry.'

'But I hadn't. I found it by accident.'

'I know that now. And then, Jenny, what happened then?'

'I couldn't just leave things as they were,' she explained, 'I wrote to the Forestry Department asking about Neil, and I received a letter from them saying they'd never heard about him.'

'And that had you puzzled.' He was grinning.

'Yes. I realised I'd misjudged you. I knew the

medallion was Neil's, but I also knew he was not a forester. I began to think up all sorts of ways the medallion could have got into your cottage. I thought perhaps Neil had done something awful . . .'

' I made you do a lot of thinking,' he grinned.

' Yes, Ross, you did. I began to think I'd got the whole thing terribly muddled. I wanted to come and tell you. And now . . . now it seems I didn't have it muddled at all.'

' No.' There was a trace of amusement in his voice. ' You never were muddle-headed, Jenny.'

' Ross, why are you making me do all this talking?' she asked.

' Because I wanted to be certain why you came. I wanted to be clear about your motives. Oh, I know,' a sheen of devilment lit his eyes, ' my own motives are so suspect that I've an awful lot of cheek.'

' You have,' she said spiritedly.

' I had a reason for doing this this way. And I wanted to be certain that the reason you came today was because you did not distrust me.'

' I've never done that,' she said steadily.

' No,' he said a little wonderingly, ' I realise that now. I just hope it's not too late . . . that I haven't made you too angry.' He sucked on his pipe. ' All right, Jenny, my explanation is long overdue. I'll give it to you now.' He looked thoughtfully into the fire while she waited with bated breath.

' I think I should begin at the time when Mother and I left the village. Were you too young to realise the cloud my father was under?'

' No,' she told him. ' I only know there was a trial.'

'How much do you remember?'

'I know it was awful.' She remembered the conversations that stopped whenever she came near. The way people would look at Neil, as if he too had done something wrong. The hushed, delighted whispers. Neil's unhappiness. Only Jenny's parents had never made Neil unwelcome, but had gone on treating him as a friend. 'I didn't really understand what happened,' she said now. Though her parents had been kind, they had never discussed the affair with her, perhaps because they had thought her too young to understand. 'I never believed it was true,' she added.

'Oh, it was true, all of it.' He was quiet a long time. Seeing the pain in his eyes, she knew it still affected him, and her heart went out to him. She longed to put out her hand to stroke his hair. With the old Neil she would not have thought twice about doing it, but this was not Neil. This was Ross.

'It was all true,' he said again presently. 'My mother discovered the whole thing only when it was in the newspapers. She stood by him right through the trial. But afterwards . . . Afterwards, as you know, we went away. We couldn't have stayed.'

'Why couldn't you have?'

'Because village life didn't permit it. Too many people who pointed fingers, who thought we were tainted with the same kind of tar.'

'Where did you go?' she asked.

'To London for a while. London is so big. Nobody was concerned about us. Nobody cared. And then . . . my father died. I never saw him again after the trial.'

'Oh, Ross!' Then her hand did go out to him. Her eyes filled with tears.

He took her hand in his, smoothing the fingers gently, absently. 'It doesn't hurt any more. One day Mother met a man. He was good to us. It didn't seem to matter to him what my father had done. He asked my mother to marry him.' He paused, then said, without expression, 'His name was Terence Sundy.'

'Oh!' Things were beginning to be a little clearer.

'Terence adopted me. He was wonderful to us both. We'd been wanting to make a new life, and it was so much easier with a new name. It was soon after Mother and Terence got married that I began to be called Ross. Ross was my grandfather's name.'

'I never knew that,' she murmured.

'No. So you see, Jenny, I *am* Ross Sundy. Rightly or wrongly, it's the way I think of myself.'

'I understand. But you've changed, Ross. I didn't recognise you. Even now—now that I know who you are—I find it hard to believe. Just the eyes—those are the same. But I didn't realise it until now.'

'We were in a car crash,' Ross said matter-of-factly. 'Mother and Terence were killed.'

'Oh, Ross!' Again her hand went out to him.

'I was badly hurt. I was in hospital for months. There was plastic surgery. It's no wonder you didn't recognise me, I was so changed after it all.'

'Your scar?' she queried.

'That happened in the forest—a falling tree. So you see, Jenny, my face has changed so much it would have been even stranger if you had known me.'

'But the Stewarts,' she pointed out. 'They knew you.'

'No, they didn't. I spoke to *them*. I met them one day in the forest. Naturally they didn't know me, but I was so glad to see people from home that I blurted out who I was. You should have seen their astonishment!'

'Ross . . .' She struggled with the emotions that seethed within her. 'That first day, when you met me in the forest . . . I'd been so much closer to you than Les and Sandra. Why didn't you tell me?'

'I haven't got round to telling you the reason for that yet,' he said softly, 'but I will.'

'Did you know me?' she asked.

'The moment you lifted your head.' He stroked her hand. 'When I saw those violet eyes looking into mine I knew I'd found my Jenny.'

'I haven't changed, then?'

'Yes, you've changed.' He touched her face, his fingers tracing the skin beneath the eyes and around the mouth. 'These are new, Jenny. And these. These are lines put into your face by grief and work. Oh, yes, Jenny, you've changed. When I knew you you were a little girl. Now you've become a woman. But the eyes . . . Only one person I know has eyes that look like violets with the dew still on them.'

'Oh, Ross!' Tears stung her lids. When he spoke like this it made things only worse, made the imminent parting even more difficult.

'Don't cry,' he said.

'I'm not crying.' She took the hanky he held out

185

to her and dabbed at her eyes. 'Why didn't you tell me who you were? You still haven't told me. If I hadn't heard you talking just now, when you thought I was asleep, I might never have known.'

'I didn't tell you,' he said very slowly, 'because I didn't want it to happen that way.'

'I don't know what you're talking about,' she said in bewilderment.

'Don't you, Jenny?' He began to stroke her hand again. 'That first day, when I saw you in the forest, I was so shocked that I hid behind my new name and appearance. I needed time to think, to evaluate what I was feeling. And then . . . then I decided to leave things as they were for the time being.'

'But why?'

'Because, Jenny, whatever you were going to feel for me, it had to be for me—Ross Sundy—not for Neil Donaldson.'

'But, Ross, you *are* Neil Donaldson. Ross *and* Neil. You're both.'

'Not to you, Jenny. Neil Donaldson is the boy you knew when you were a child. Ross is a grown man, a different person altogether.'

'I think I understand . . . vaguely.' Her eyes were shining, trying to grasp the implication of what she thought he was trying to say.

'You came here looking for Neil—for a boy you'd played with when you were little. I thought, Jenny, that if you knew who I was, you might grow to . . . to care for me. And then I would never have known if your feelings were not just a continuation of the way you'd felt for the boy you remembered.'

'How could you not have known, Ross?' she whispered.

'You were so adamant that you must find him.' He laughed and sucked on his pipe. 'The way I keep saying "him" . . . it's as if I have a split personality. But I had to be sure, Jenny. Can you see that?'

'I wish I'd known,' she sighed.

'No. You see, my darling, in your grief and loneliness I thought you were turning to someone who was just a memory, and I wanted more than that.'

'But it wasn't like that,' she protested. 'I just knew Neil was here, and I wanted to find him. I felt there was some mystery and I wanted to clear it up.'

'I never managed to convince you on that score, did I?'

'At times you nearly did,' she confessed.

'Really? And then there was Andrew. I saw the way you danced with him, kissed him . . .'

'He kissed me. He was trying to make you jealous,' Jenny said earnestly.

'You said that once before.'

'It was true. Besides,' she countered with spirit, 'what about Ann?'

'What has Ann to do with this?'

'She wasn't happy that I was seeing you,' Jenny said carefully. 'I thought perhaps . . .'

'Ann is a pretty girl,' Ross said matter-of-factly. 'It can be lonely here in the mountains. We spent quite a bit of time together—it was only natural. But she meant no more to me than a pleasant companion.'

'I see.'

'I don't think we need worry about Ann.' He chuckled. 'From what I hear she's taken up with your old swain. Andrew still has some time at the hotel. They'll be quite happy to spend it together.'

'Yes, but Ross . . .' there was still one thing that worried her, 'why could you tell me now who you are? What changed—what made things different?'

'You told me certain things,' he said without expression.

'What things?'

'Jenny,' he grinned wickedly, 'has anyone ever told you that you talk in your sleep?'

'I do?' She clapped a hand over her mouth in consternation. 'Have I been talking?'

'You have, Jin-Jin.'

'What did I say?'

'I'll tell you some time.'

'Now?' she pleaded.

'No.'

'When, then?'

'How about,' he began teasingly, but with a look in his eyes that made her heart skip a bit, 'on our wedding day?'

'Oh, Ross . . . Ross!' The tears were falling now as he bent down and put his arms around her. 'I'm going away. I must take Mrs Ramsden back to England. One of the reasons I came was to say goodbye.'

'You'll come back?' He was holding her tightly.

'Do you really want me to?' she whispered against his chest.

'I love you, Jin-Jin.' He was nuzzling his mouth against her face. 'I loved you when you were small. I fell in love with you when I saw you in the forest.'

'Oh, Ross!' She felt as if the happiness was almost too much to bear.

'Jenny.' He kissed her then, strongly and passionately, the way she had always dreamed he would. 'You'll come back? You won't be too lonely here?'

'I could never be lonely with you, my darling, wherever in the world we might be.' Ross *was* her world. Ross and the mountains and the forest and the rivers. What more could any girl want?